Praise for Dendrites

T0266640

"What possibilities do p
live in terrible condition.
Kafka's too, unites the lives of the characters who
inhabit this extraordinary novel. Living on the margins
is not a choice, but a circumstance and a fate. Kallia
Papadaki explores the margins these Greek emigrants
lived in with profound insight and empathy. The result
is a wise and sensitive novel, but not only that—Kallia
is also a virtuoso in the art of storytelling, which is,
increasingly, a rarity these days. *Dendrites* is a
cohesive novel, offering abundant literary prose and
a perfect narrative structure."
RONALDO MENÉNDEZ

"The winner of the 2017 European Union Prize for
Literature vindicates all the female voices in European
literature, who are often silenced by a lack of translation into other languages of the EU."
Vogue

"A novel about disillusion and everyday failures."
ELLE

"A wonderful debut. Don't let it pass you by."
Qué Leer

"In living organisms, the word dendrites refers to the
branches of nerve cells. Here, the reference is to
branching in general. The novel is like a tree, whose
twenty chapters are the branches, each tirelessly
described with the precision of a sociologist, by an

author who is as much a screenwriter as a novelist and who thinks in terms of cinematographic images."
Le Soir

"With great ease, the novel combines narration with the characters' inner monologues, thanks to Papadaki's peculiar poetic and versatile prose, which hardly uses any punctuation beyond commas. *Dendrites* is an ambitious, courageous, and sincere work of literature, as well as a social document of European migration to the USA."
Todo Literatura

"One of the best Greek novels of the last few years. Truly exceptional."
Lifo Magazine

"A deeply poetic book of great beauty, which will leave an indelible mark."
Books Journal

"The book's two female characters belong next to the classic characters of Greek literature."
Amagi

"Sad as the blues, existential, profoundly political, contemporary and timely … Simply extraordinary. Had it been written in English, it would have caused a stir."
Le Monde diplomatique

"*Dendrites* might be the best Greek novel of the summer."
Propaganda

"In this magnificent and evocative novel, Kallia Papadaki reconstructs with great poetic prowess the story
of a Greek family who emigrate to North America."
ABC Cultural

"The female characters, in all the different eras of the
story, are fiercely determined."
Aullido

"*Dendrites* is an existentialist generational chronicle, of
surprising psychological clarity, despite its fragmen-
tary structure."
Indienauta

"One of our three recommended translated novels for
the 2020 festive season."
Llanuras

"For the daring with which Papadaki launches us into
this story of genesis and exodus from person to person,
from era to era, from decision to decision, and for her
insistence that all things—losses, and especially
successes—are impermanent, we can only recom-
mend her novel, *Dendrites*."
Culturamas

"In a prose that avoids punctuation and aspires to flow
like a litany, Kallia Papadaki wants to show that this
history is, like all histories, on the verge of disappearing, and is, like all histories, beautiful and complex in
an irreducibly unique way."
El correo

"If there is something that unites us, in addition to nationalities, eras, and circumstances, it is our capacity to keep moving forward despite all the dreams we witness being shattered one by one."
El Confidencial

"Papadaki has written a fascinating book."
Book Press

"Papadaki handles her material skillfully, building a solid narrative with cinematic mastery."
Fractal

"*Dendrites* captures no less than sixty years of family history, spanning three generations: father, son, stepdaughter. The implacable hand of destiny consumes it all, eliminating the individuality of every life like that of the ice crystals, those dendrites of a unique and irreproducible beauty that melt without a trace. A splendid novel."
Boulevard Literario blog

"The striking circular structure of the novel whisks us off into the dramatic history of the Greek emigrants (and it could be about any nationality, really), of their attempts to get ahead in the United States, and their struggle to get a whiff of the 'American dream.' The story, stretching from the early twentieth century to the eighties, is personified in the figure of Andonis Cambanis and his son Vasilis. An elegy to resilience."
La Rossa Bookshop

DENDRITES

KALLIA PAPADAKI

DENDRITES

Translated from the Greek
by Karen Emmerich

WORLD EDITIONS
New York

Published in the USA in 2024 by World Editions NY LLC, New York

World Editions
New York

Printed by Lightning Source, USA

Library of Congress Cataloging in Publication Data is available

ISBN 978-1-64286-136-5

First published as *Δενδρίτες* in Greece in 2015 by Polis Editions, Athens. This edition is published by arrangement with Kallia Papadaki in conjunction with their duly appointed agent Marotte et Compagnie Agence littéraire, France.

This publication was supported by the Hellenic Ministry of Culture and Sports and the Hellenic Foundation for Culture within the framework of the GreekLit programme.

GreekLit.

Company: worldeditions.org
Facebook: @WorldEditionsInternationalPublishing
Instagram: @WorldEdBooks
TikTok: @worldeditions_tok
Twitter: @WorldEdBooks
YouTube: World Editions

To my parents,
Antigone and Manolis

Author's Note

Camden, New Jersey, and its neighboring city of Philadelphia, Pennsylvania, are separated by the Delaware River and joined by the Benjamin Franklin and Walt Whitman Bridges. Camden was a melting pot of immigrants for generations, while industry was booming and there were plenty of jobs to go around. Things changed after the end of World War II. Industries relocated to the Western States and Mexico. Jobs dried up and new waves of Puerto Rican and African American migrants flooded the city in search of a better life. In September 1949, in East Camden, the war veteran Howard Unruh shot and killed thirteen people in the space of twelve minutes. It was the first recorded mass murder in the history of the United States. In the years that followed, three mayors of Camden were tried and imprisoned for corruption. In 2012 the city had the highest crime rate of the entire country. Today about forty percent of the population continues to live below the poverty line. All this belongs to the realm of known truth. Otherwise, any similarity to people, names, or situations is entirely by chance, and bears no relation to reality.

"... time has run its course ... this life is no more than a fading reflection of an event beyond recall ..."

W.G. SEBALD, ON JORGE LOUIS BORGES'S "TLÖN, UQBAR, ORBIS TERTIUS"

I

the autumn wind
has torn the telegram and more
from mother's hand
NICK VIRGILIO

Minnie unravels her two truncated braids and gathers her hair into an asymmetrical ponytail. A tear
rolls down each flushed cheek and she quickly wipes
them away with her sleeve before anyone notices.
There's a woolen knot of frustration lodged in her
throat, things are all wrong, middle school is a
waste of time, her classmates are idiots, her brother
is a bully who steals her allowance, and today, when
she finally got up the courage to fight back, he
grabbed her craft scissors and sawed off half her left
braid, and as if that weren't bad enough, he said if
she breathed a word to their mother she'd regret it,
and Minnie knows perfectly well that his threats are
never empty, so she brought the scissors to school,
stood in front of the mirror in the girls' room, and
chopped off the bottom of her right braid, too, to

bring it even with the left. Her mother isn't stupid, she's sure to ask what happened, and Minnie will have to invent some story. A third tear trickles down, which this time Minnie swallows.

But before she can really digest it, a shadowy figure appears in front of her, a blond girl a head taller than Minnie, backlit by the soft, hazy October light. "Got a smoke?" she asks, then watches quizzically as Minnie shrivels into her corner. Minnie doesn't smoke, in fact the one time she put a cigarette in her mouth and pretended to inhale her mother slapped her, leaving a bright red finger mark between mouth and ear. She can still remember the sting and the salty tears that sprang to her eyes, and this distant memory dredges up a forgotten emotion as she takes a deep, sharp breath to calm the distress bubbling up inside, threatening to overflow. "Never mind, forget it, it's no big deal," the blond girl mumbles indifferently, sitting down beside her, crossing her arms and splaying her legs out on the warm cement. The girl secures the perimeter with her eyes, pulls a half-melted bar of chocolate out of her back pocket, pops a piece in her mouth, licks her fingers, then wipes her hands on her worn jeans as her teeth turn the same wheaty color as her permanently sunburned skin. "Want some?" she murmurs, waving the chocolate bar at Minnie, who shyly breaks off a tiny corner and carefully lets it melt in her mouth as if testing her limits. She's kind of squeamish about germs, but she does it—she dares—holding her breath for a minute before swallowing, her mouth tightly sealed, because germs can't survive without oxygen, can they?

"Your name's Leto, right?" Minnie says hesitantly, since what she'd like most of all is to be left alone. She's in no mood for a Q&A and in the past six weeks at this new school she probably hasn't spoken more than five sentences to another soul. It's all about the impression you make, what you wear, where you live, where you go on vacation, and Minnie knows she'd give all the wrong answers to her classmates' silent but insistent questions. But now it's the other girl's face that's darkening under her dirty blond hair and unruly mess of freckles, and as she stares down at her sneakers, Minnie gathers the courage to open her mouth a crack, just enough to reveal her two missing front teeth, and asks "Where's the name Leto from, anyway?"—and the girl with the mottled freckles bristles and shoves her, hard, then stands up, shakes out her limbs, and lopes off across the schoolyard, hands in her pockets as Minnie wipes her eyes, sniffs, takes a deep breath, and gives a swift kick with her shabby tennis shoe to an annoying pebble on the pavement that was just asking for it.

The blond girl is in fact named Leto, which isn't a big deal, some of her classmates have names just as strange, awkward, and hard to pronounce, but Leto's happens to carry with it a shadowy satellite, an extra piece she's been dragging around like the tail of a comet since birth, an asterisk, a cruel footnote to her already ridiculous name. What on earth had her mother been thinking, sticking her with a middle name that would dog her every step for her entire life? On official documents and in the school register she's Leto 68 Kambanis Miller, and no matter how hard she tries to ignore it, to move past it, to let herself get swept up in the carefree play of early adolescence, it's always there, like this morning when some oblivious teacher decided to make a joke about it, inviting her classmates' ridicule and snide laughter. She doesn't want to be different, to stand out, she never has, and at the sensitive age of twelve her freakish height and already developed body make her conspicuous enough as it is, what she wants is to belong, to be the same as everyone else, part of an indistinguishable mass, and how is she supposed to blend in with kids who have normal, boring names when she's dragging that stupid number around all the time?

She hates her 68 with a passionate, undying grudge, despises any number that even comes close. It's no accident that history class is her nightmare, she's always getting dates confused, sometimes on purpose and sometimes not, she's chewed her mother out a million times for saddling her with such a strange name, and for pinning her under the weight of that number, too—a number that will always haunt her. What does Leto care what 1968 meant for her mother, or for humanity at large? Leto's only mistake, which isn't even entirely her fault, was to come into the world just before her due date, landing in her mother's arms on December 31, 1968, forever doomed to remind Susan Miller of all the experiences she never got to have, since when Leto was still a baby her mother met Basil Kambanis, Leto's stepfather and adoptive father, married him, and even went into business with him. They'd both saved up some money from their wages, working and flirting on the floor of the Campbell Soup factory, and decided to buy and renovate the 44, once a popular Polish diner in the neighborhood of Cramer Hill where a badly painted mural of the poet Adam Mickiewicz presided over the lunch counter, still a symbol of tolerance and reconciliation in the 1940s when the place was built, trumpeting leftist democratic ideals along the eastern waterfront of a deeply conservative city that had come of age and spread its wings thanks to first- and second-generation Republican immigrants—a city divided into quiet ethnic neighborhoods whose residents tended not to mix outside the melting pot of the factory, and if someone escaped the confines of their neighborhood and headed to the Delaware River or to the northwest corner of the city it was because they'd finally made something of themselves, managed to put a roof over their head and a few dollars in their pocket, the American dream was the common language they all shared, a language that made successes sound shinier and talked circles around failure, consigning the poor to the purgatory of the not-yet-arrived.

Her parents had met at the Campbell Soup factory, where a twenty-four-year-old Susan stacked cans on a conveyer belt eight hours a day, six days a week, and where, at twenty-eight, Basil was a manager, responsible for nearly a thousand people per shift, plus hundreds of thousands of identical cans of concentrated tomato soup. Susan had once been a student at Ohio State University, but a year before she was set to earn her degree in political science with a focus on political economy, she fell in love with the hippie son of an industrialist, dropped out, and followed him across the country, all the way to Haight-Ashbury, San Francisco. Their romance lasted a year and a half—one summer at a commune and two mild winters on the streets panhandling love from passersby and handing out flowers in return, until Leto and Woodstock came between them, and the harsh winters of the Northeast, which were nothing to laugh at, and so after the rain and mud of the festival they limped their separate ways, Scott back to the family hearth to enroll, like it or not, at Berkeley, where the western wing of the Department of Zoology carried the name of his great-grandfather, Johnson Jr., while Susan, who had bumped heads with her Protestant working-class father and wasn't going back to Columbus Stinking Ohio even if the whole world were to catch fire, boarded a dilapidated Greyhound bus in the middle of the night and arrived at dawn in Camden, New Jersey, home of RCA Victor, where her kid brother worked. Two months later she met Basil, and they were married at City Hall within another six, just as Leto was celebrating her fourteenth pudgy month in this world—and no matter how much they insisted it had been love at first sight, the only one around to hear was her brother, who was less interested in his sister's happiness than in the fact that he now had two fewer mouths to feed. It didn't matter that he, like Basil, was a manager; tough times were coming, and though hope still charged the atmosphere with illusions, you could sense the inevitable knocking like death on your neighbors' doors, could see it in the abandoned factories and deserted homes whose number increased exponentially from month to month.

First the New York Shipbuilding Corporation gave way, fell to its knees, dragging two and a half thousand workers down with it. The books couldn't be balanced without new orders coming in, and what wartime industry had built with such zeal was quickly destroyed by popular demands for a new, better, and more peaceful world; and a year or two later, shortly after Nixon assumed the reins of power, the RCA Victor plant closed too, as its mascot, the music-loving terrier named Nipper, set its sights on the cheap labor of Mexico. Management blamed the union, which was on indefinite strike for better wages, while the union blamed management for putting profits above everything else, and the city was suddenly bereft of jobs. Five thousand people in a city of ninety thousand were laid off in a single week, and thus, midway through 1970, the diner—which Basil and Susan had renamed the Ariadne, though you could still make out a faded Mickiewicz beneath the off-white columns painted above a colorful Greek salad and mouthwatering gyro plate on the wall— ceased being what it was and had promised to be, as a slowdown in the economy and the endless war in Vietnam drove the recently thriving city into crisis: its residents lost their trust in one another, the threads holding neighborhoods together unraveled, and whoever could afford to leave moved to the burgeoning suburbs. First the Jews, then the Italians and Greeks, until only Leto's parents seemed to remain immutably optimistic, and in their optimism entirely unwilling to move: they dug in their heels like mules and watched their savings blow away in the wind and their dreams vanish one by one.

Leto doesn't really care about all that, her parents had made their bed and now they'd have to lie in it—only their spineless decisions affect her, too. They dreamed of a perfect world, brought her into a society that was supposedly changing for the better, but she calls bullshit. The only thing in her life that reliably makes her happy and has any clear meaning is soccer, two well-defined goals on freshly cut grass, the unambiguous rules governing the game, the ball spinning over the field like an apple of discord among twenty-two tough pairs of legs, defense and tackles, especially tackles—goals aren't her forte, so she ignores them, along with everything else that annoys her.

For Leto, East Camden Middle School is a necessary evil that at some point she'll shake free of, certainly by the impending end of puberty, if not sooner. She's decided that all her suffering, including over her unfortunate name, stems from the awkward, sensitive phase of adolescence and its many injustices, the annoying blond fuzz on her thighs and calves, the close-fitting bra that makes her feel like she can't breathe, the stupid allergic asthma that brings her to her knees with no warning, like during that game last spring when the pollen was everywhere, all of nature going wild. They were playing Cooper Point Middle School and her team was up one to zero with two minutes left in the second half when a forward from the other team slipped by their defense, and just as Leto was in the middle of a heroic sprint, coming in from the left, about to execute the most important slide tackle of her life to date, winning a regional trophy for the team and maybe even the plaque for most valuable player, suddenly she could barely breathe, she doubled over, her face went red, and the ball rolled right by her as if in slow motion, followed by the other team's center forward, who seemed to be moving at a stroll, dribbling unsteadily toward the goalie who had come forward in a risky maneuver, and scoring probably out of pure luck into the empty goal. The game went into overtime and Leto watched the extra half hour from the bench, cursing her delicate genes and all the weed she had smoked in her mother's womb, while her team, down to ten players with no subs, lost the trophy and she lost the plaque she'd been dreaming of. "These things happen," her coach said in her dumb Oklahoma accent in the locker room, but they only ever happened to her, and Leto wanted to shout "Only to me," but in the end she kept her mouth shut, slumped down on a bench in the corner, and clenched her hands into fists, sinking her nails into her palms so she wouldn't smash everything in sight, wouldn't ruin the trophy ceremony, but most of all so she wouldn't cry in front of her teammates, who were already shooting her dismissive looks that obviously referenced the game's final outcome. And now, today, she's reliving the whole episode, when the shrill cries of her classmates—running through the schoolyard chasing an unfortunate alley cat with a wound from an air gun on its back—bring her back to the present, to the bell ringing for the next period, to the inhaler she pulls from her pocket, a deep puff to help her endure her intolerable life and her impending American History class.

Sitting at the back of the room, Leto shifts her legs, trying to get comfortable at her desk as Ms. Gardener rattles on about the golden age of the roaring '20s, when growth was synonymous with consumption and an industrial city's affluence was measured by the number of smoke-spewing chimneys that dotted its horizon, or the swarms of workers, locals and immigrants alike, who buzzed through the streets each morning, human caravans setting out at dawn to earn their daily bread. Ms. Gardener moves up and down the aisles between the desks, dragging her chunky sandals over the worn tiles of the floor, hypnotizing all twenty-five students with her slow, borderline catatonic dance, her body a pendulum swinging back and forth on its own momentum, slower and slower each time, and soon the swinging will stop and this tiny woman in her sixties will relax, letting her shoulders roll forward, and Leto will wonder if all that knowledge is what makes bodies stoop and hunch over time, and as she disappears into these random thoughts, Ms. Gardener will touch her gently on the shoulder and whisper in her ear, like a distant echo of an inevitable future, "Don't slouch, or your back will stay that way," and then vanish just as quickly as she came, back up to the board, as the bell rings and twenty-five chairs scrape the floor, screeching almost in unison.

Leto slips quickly out of the room, hefting her backpack onto shoulders she squares in an exaggerated attempt not to hunch, though soon enough she forgets and walks on with her head bowed, lost in daydreams, book bag bouncing against her back with each hurried step. She wants to get home before dark, not that she's scared, but a week ago, a Monday just like today, some assholes from Woodrow Wilson High ambushed a group of kids from the middle school basketball team and beat them up for no reason, just for kicks, so she picks up speed, trying not to think about all the bad things that could possibly happen, her mother says your mind can do the most damage of all, can imagine the worst, can conjure up secret paths where there's really nothing but wild, dense foliage, can invent things in the heat of the moment that you'll end up paying for all your life—"You know what I mean, honey"—and though Leto doesn't, in fact, know precisely what Susan means, she's a quick study, and soon enough she'll get the drift, catch on to the deeper meaning of this all-powerful, eternally present motherly filter.

The sun sets lazily behind the city of Camden as Leto trips and bends down to tie her shoelace. Across the way a school bus trundles down the avenue with the slogan *Equal Opportunity in Education* on its flank, and she catches sight of Minnie's face pressed to one of the windows, framed by those dark, curly, chopped-off braids, staring off into the distance, toward the Delaware River and beyond, toward Philadelphia where her father lives, he left when she was a baby, she never knew him, the only image she still has of him is of a pair of dusty, faded boots that she found in the attic, size 14, which she turned into flowerpots, filling them with soil and fertilizer and planting a handful of beans for a science experiment for school.

Minnie lives in a disreputable part of town, full of

faded, crumbling gray stone houses that have all been worn down by time in the same way, so there's a sort of harmony in their pervasive ugliness. The damaged stone doesn't seem strange, it's as if time has made it wiser, as if the ramshackle shells of these houses carry the past almost with reverence, bearing witness to how human ambition can founder in the stream of events. It's a neighborhood where residents coexist with ruins, having learned to live with decline, and only now in winter when night falls early might you feel scared, when the decrepit buildings are shrouded in a mist of darkness, and their outlines regain something of their former spiky splendor—and to banish the softness of night that falls like a balm, covering the worn stone, people become monsters, lest they dream of deserving something better and buck against their miserable fate. Minnie climbs down from the bus, shrugs her backpack on, gives a quick wave to her Mexican friend, the driver Miguel, nicknamed Octopus, wraps her thin jacket around her body, and fixes her gaze straight ahead as she runs along Newton Creek, which hugs the edge of Morgan Village as it flows westward toward the Delaware River, whose humidity oppresses the city year round—and in summer blood-sucking mosquitoes feed on the stagnant waters of the Cooper River and the human shipwrecks who live on its banks.

"You're home early," her mother calls from the kitchen as Minnie, out of breath, drops her bag in the hallway of their ground-floor apartment, rushes into the living room, picks up the remote, and turns on the TV. "Rats," she says, because they still haven't announced when the next episode of *Dallas* will air, and she's dying to find out who shot J.R., it's been six months since the season finale last March and the question still hangs in the air. Now it's nearly November and the culprit still hasn't been revealed. The whole summer was spent in speculation, then September brought Minnie new hope, the new season was about to begin, things would fall into place, but to her terrible luck the writers' guild was in the middle of an indefinite strike, in September the channel said October, and when October rolled around they said mid-November, viewers were up in arms, and in an effort to keep interest alive the producers at CBS threw oil on the fire, parading teasers across TV screens all over the country with versions of who the would-be murderer might have been, and the rumors swelled again, betting parlors got in on the action, but for Minnie the teasers just made things worse, half the characters had motives, though all summer long she was pretty sure it was J.R.'s mother, Miss Ellie Ewing, he'd put that poor woman through hell and no one can hurt you the way family can, the closer the relation the crueler the pain, like in September when her big brother Pete raised his air gun and aimed straight for her left shoulder, and when the pellet hit her Minnie let out a scream loud enough for the whole neighborhood to hear, and he laughed and apologized, he hadn't meant to, it was an accident, shit happens, and the pain narrowed Minnie's lovely eyes into buttonholes, blurry with sudden tears, and then she knew for sure that it must have been Miss Ellie.

"They said it'll air on the twenty-first."

Minnie turns her head and sees her mother standing in the doorway chewing a slice of fried plantain, Minnie thinks plantains are gross, she's always found the taste and texture disgusting ever since someone first shoved one in her mouth when she was a baby, and no matter how much her mother—impatient, domineering Louisa from San Juan—argues that they're low in sugar and high in potassium, and that she should get over her pickiness and learn to accept what's good for her, that it's just another childish notion she'll live to regret, Minnie's never changed her opinion, and as she stares at the television with her back turned to Louisa, about to ask what they're having for dinner, she's starving, she suddenly feels the atmosphere crackle with electricity, and just as light moves faster than sound, the words follow right afterward, breaking like a thunderclap—"Dammit, what did you do to your hair?"—and to drive home the point, Louisa's fingers, greasy from cooking, reach out and tug on what's left of her braids, as if tugging could bring back what's gone.

It's almost eleven and there's no sign of Pete. Her mother is pacing back and forth in the living room, and Minnie, wrapped in her wool baby blanket in one corner of the sofa, is pretending to be engrossed in some particularly tricky math homework. "What time is it now?" Louisa asks for the umpteenth time, and then, neither expecting nor receiving an answer, "When did you see him last?" And Minnie, eyes still on her book, mumbles, "Mom, I told you, he was at school today," and Louisa walks to the front door, swings it open, and balances on the few square feet of sidewalk outside as if debating whether or not she should cross the street, as if the street isn't a street at all but a wild river rushing madly past, and her uneasy figure appears now in silhouette, tottering spookily between the lace curtains, her shadow magnified on the wall, floating above the sofa and Minnie's head like a piece of bad news. Now it's after midnight. Louisa is at the kitchen table, head resting on her arms, Minnie is dozing on the sofa, and between them sits the silent telephone, no one knows anything, his two best friends have been home for hours, the police have no information but tell them not to worry, if they hear anything they'll be in touch—and the receiver sits there silently in its cradle, as otherworldly as the scenes Louisa imagines and Minnie dreams.

It's nearly dawn and there's still no sign of Pete. Louisa hasn't budged at all, her body stuck at the bottom of a seesaw, like a weight on a scale that's missing its pair. Minnie sleeps fitfully on the sofa wrapped in her wool blanket, and sunlight creeps through the window inch by inch to illuminate all the dusty corners, yesterday's cobwebs built by industrious spiders, the smattering of crumbs on the floor, the decay and abandonment caused by a night of deep sadness, and Louisa rises listlessly from her chair, turns on a burner, and mechanically starts to fry eggs, thin strips of bacon, and bread slathered with margarine and sprinkled with sugar.

Behind her stands a sleepy Minnie, hair mussed and empty stomach gurgling. She pulls at her mother's faded robe but gets no response, then quietly asks, "Mom, what time is it," not wanting to startle Louisa with an ill-timed question because her mother looks like a ghost, her shoulders have hunched with exhaustion, her body seems nearly concave, as if she's suddenly shed all her extra pounds, as if in the course of a single night her clothes have come to hang limply on her frame. "What time is it?" Minnie repeats, and a hypnotized Louisa opens the drawer, takes out placemats frayed with use and time and says, "Time for breakfast, that's what time," and out of habit lays the table for three.

They eat together, the neighboring houses still shrouded in morning mist, the surrounding roads sunk in stubborn silence; in half an hour everything will be different, Louisa knows that once day breaks nothing will be the same and she's placed all her remaining hope in this in-between time when her thoughts can stretch out long and gather again like shadows, filling the tiny space of waiting still left before the news she's expecting arrives, she knows her son is mixed up in gangs and drugs, the ladies from the Baptist church told her, trying to bring her around, pull her onto the Lord's path, and for a few weeks she wavered, wondering what good it really did to keep her distance, to insist on her difference, to resist the dictates of the local community, but in the end she simply had no faith in second or third chances that fall like manna from heaven to fill the bellies of those who have gone hungry for years.

Minnie gets her backpack ready and runs to catch the school bus, Louisa draws the curtains, pulls over a kitchen stool and sits in front of the window, Minnie chases after the bus that's pulling away, Louisa sits and listens to the sound of her own breathing, and to a creeping procession of belated *whys*, *if onlys*, and *maybes* that surround her body, pounding her from all sides, Minnie loses sight of the bus as it picks up speed on the avenue, becoming a tiny trembling speck on the edge of a deep red horizon as Louisa takes a few sharp, deep breaths, clutches her chest, and tumbles to the floor, because her heart no longer wants to inhabit that body, and her clenched, raised fist is proof of her final, fruitless struggle.

II

I dream'd in a dream, I saw a city invincible to the attacks
*   of the whole of the rest of the earth;*
I dream'd that was the new City of Friends;
Nothing was greater there than the quality of robust love—
*   it led the rest;*
It was seen every hour in the actions of the men of that city,
And in all their looks and words.

WALT WHITMAN

He grits his teeth with pain, cold sweat streams into
his palms, there's no way he'll emerge unscathed,
and yet the bullets flew right by him, missed their
target, didn't defile his flesh. He tries to breathe,
something in his chest is suffocating him, a stifled
complaint that seems unable to emerge. Fallen there
on the ground, he raises his eyes and sees a pool of
blood ten feet to his right, a rigid body blocking the
narrow sidewalk before him, onlookers gesturing,
and a buzzing sound pierces his ears. With his right
hand he gropes his body to locate the source of the
pain, but there's no wound, and that frightens him

even more, the thoughts running through his mind start to snowball—his bedridden wife, his son too young to look after himself, his business in debt—and Antonis Kambanis blacks out, returning in his mind to when he was nineteen years old, a stranger among strangers.

It took the ocean liner twenty-two days to reach its destination, and when the *Patris* spewed its crush of one thousand three hundred souls onto Ellis Island it was November 7 and a slushy snow was falling. He spat on the ground three times as a kind of exorcism, a promise he'd made to his mother, who had strange ideas about the power of the human will and always said that only spit and grit will help you find your footing and get ahead in a new place. The moment he eventually set foot in Manhattan, a tall, bony guy from Rhodes sidled up, offering to find him a job, for a fee of course, swore up and down that the paltry sum Antonis had brought from his village on the island of Nisyros was plenty to make a start, and after shoving the cash in the pocket of his wide-cuffed pants, he found Antonis a room to share with four others at a small boardinghouse, which seemed more like a tin shack to Antonis, and arranged a time for them to meet the next day a few blocks away, wrote down the intersection on a piece of paper, *Broadway and Franklin*, and told him that if he wasn't there when Antonis arrived he should ask for a man named Smerlis, then he repeated the name, giving the *r* a good roll, clapped Antonis conspiratorially on the shoulder, and left as quickly as he'd come, assuring him just before he vanished from sight that he'd come to the right country at exactly the right time, that here in America there were good-paying, steady jobs for bright, ambitious young men like him, then he winked and hurried off into the thick darkness of the city that never slept, whose dirty, disreputable alleyways were already alive with the sounds of night.

The next day the guy from Rhodes didn't show, and Antonis quickly realized that no Smerlis was expecting him either. There was no one on the corner but a group of scrawny kids, no older than twelve or thirteen, squatting with brushes and tins of shoe polish and shouting "Three cents a pair, five for a fella and his lady," and every now and then shining the muddy shoes of some passerby. The whole city of New York was one vast construction site, public works and skyscrapers rising up to house a crowded dream, a dream that lost its luster down here amid the squat shacks and swampy streets, and Antonis Kambanis, who had now placed all his hopes in a miracle, couldn't believe that his twenty dollars had gone up in a puff of smoke, he'd barely set foot in the New World and had already been taken for a fool, he couldn't believe what an idiot he'd been, and he wracked his brain for some kind of solution, but of course he didn't speak the language, all he knew was *good morning*, *excuse me*, and *thank you*, phrases he rolled around awkwardly in his mouth like piping hot food, so how was he supposed to explain to anyone what had befallen him? Standing there in his confusion he caught the eye of an Italian mobster out patrolling his turf, ten blocks along Broadway and five to the west, a rectangle that ended at Hudson

Street. He'd come to collect the shoe shiners' wages and saw this stranger hanging around who might even be a threat, who knew, and started chattering at him in Sicilian to see how much he knew and whether he had an eye for business, maybe it was his swarthy looks that suggested a possible kinship from the south of Italy. They exchanged a few phrases that went nowhere, then resorted to gestures and grimaces, and when Kambanis pulled out his Italian papers and passport—badges of a temporary paternity that, with the Treaty of Ouchy, had embraced the Dodecanese Islands since 1912—the Italian lost no time in welcoming him, promising him a place to stay and a job as long as he was willing to take care of a few loose threads in Hell's Kitchen, but Antonis Kambanis had learned his lesson, once bitten twice shy, he wasn't going to run errands for anyone ever again unless they gave him something up front for his trouble, and so the two men's paths diverged again as quickly as they had come together—though not in fact forever.

Two weeks later, on the advice and encouragement of a dishwasher from Souli in Western Greece, Antonis Kambanis found himself in the state of New Jersey, working as a welder at the Camden shipyards of the New York Shipbuilding Corporation, earning twenty cents an hour, which covered his minimal expenses—a tiny room on Sylvan Street in Morgan Village, two plates of cold food prepared the day before by his Polish landlady, and an outing each Sunday to what were for him the uncharted eastern outskirts of the city, to Cramer Hill where the language on the streets was German, or to the Jewish neighborhoods of Marlton and Parkside, bordered on one side by the meandering line of the Cooper River. And since this newcomer from Nisyros didn't yet speak much English, his walks were lonely and the coins in his pocket few, and every so often he stopped to gape like a fish at the two-story wooden houses inhabited by families of four or five, or into the windows of shops selling sweets and ice cream, or at the synagogues where clusters of Orthodox Jews milled around, dark sidelocks hanging symmetrically in front of both ears, or at restaurants that served mouth-watering potato pancakes and Ukrainian goulash.

Kambanis didn't have much to do with other Greeks, after all there weren't many and they were scattered across the city like poppies sprouting wild in the fields. There wasn't yet a church to draw them together into a few tight-knit blocks from which they could spread out again as the community grew—though nearby Philadelphia had at least two Orthodox churches and a thousand or so parishioners, and so on a Sunday different from all the rest when sleep evaded him entirely, he left the house before dawn, went down to the dock at Cooper Point, took the ferry across the Delaware River, and attended morning service at St. George's. It was September 10, 1922, the day after the Turkish capture of Smyrna, and between prayers and readings from the liturgy, three hundred shocked and anxious compatriots whispered about the events in Asia Minor, which were suddenly front-page news in the Sunday edition of *The New York Times*. Antonis had a foreboding feeling that he couldn't quite place or explain, a dark, painful knowledge that pressed on his chest, and the longer he sat with it the more certain he became that there was no turning back, that he'd have to figure out how to build a life here in this strange, foreign place, that he would never return to the island of his birth. That same morning his mother died quietly in her sleep at just fifty years old, of grief and a heart attack, and Antonis Kambanis learned three weeks after the fact that his cousins on Nisyros had taken care of the funeral, and to cover their costs were going to sell the only thing in the world he could still call his own, his family home.

He was twenty-two years old, orphaned of both parents, with no home or relations nearby, living in a city whose name carried no memories, only the present, when suddenly he experienced an entirely unexpected shift: his mother's death freed him of the guilt that had been holding him back. Kambanis had always planned on eventually returning to his native island, and he counted his savings down to the penny; every dollar that he shoved into the envelope under his mattress brought him that much closer to his mother, to the land they would buy and cultivate together, to the stone terraces they would build in their fields. Her death found him with thirty-two dollars and fifty-three cents that would never be spent on that dream, and so a week later he ducked out of work an hour early and went to the Kotlikoff department store, where he pored over the racks and shelves and window displays for a good three hours, finally settling on a nice suit and a pair of leather shoes, the first truly extravagant purchases of his life—because who cared about the money, in the mind of every American you were what you were trying to become, savings were meant to be spent, and he too needed to drum up the courage to make a break with his past and become someone, which meant becoming someone else.

Yet, though the weeks passed, he remained the very same Antonis Kambanis, perhaps because he'd always been reserved and measured, a sensible man of few words, and so the new suit hung unworn in his wardrobe as the city outside his window galloped outward in concentric circles toward the suburbs, as ornate buildings sprang up in a matter of months, music halls buzzed with dancing and a lust for life, and new immigrants poured into the region to join the boom while those who had been there longer began to demand better wages. Money changed hands and fortunes were made, women won the right to vote, Victorian morality breathed its last in speakeasies where moonshine flowed and crowds danced the Charleston and the shimmy as the end of the butchery of the Great War marked the beginning of a glorious, hopeful age.

And as neon lights flashed outside of the cinemas and entertainment halls where people lined up to revel until morning, and the reflections of those lights quivered in puddles on the streets below, Antonis Kambanis tried to understand where he'd gone wrong, why he was still living such a hardscrabble, miserable life without a shred of hope for anything more, why he could never manage to pay his rent on time, causing his landlady to greet him each morning with a sour, displeased air, and why expenses kept piling up while income was so hard to come by. He'd lasted three long winters and two fleeting summers at the shipyard, where the work was tough, the conditions harsh, and the pay not great for anyone, and worse for those who spoke broken English, and on the cusp of the fourth winter, toward the end of October, his landlady told him she'd found a better tenant, more comfortably situated and better able to pay, and she'd thank him very much if he could gather his things and shove off by the end of the week. That very morning he spent all of half an hour packing his earthly possessions into a prewar suitcase that had once belonged to his uncle, then donned his good suit for the very first time and went out into the streets, leaving two weeks' rent unpaid. It was a gray day, the kind without even a sliver of blue in the sky, low clouds mingled with smoke from the chimneys, and Antonis looked like some otherworldly figure that had lost its way in the morning mists as he circled the same few blocks with his tattered suitcase in hand, around and around, as the day dragged on and the sky finally darkened once more.

Night found him in the Central Waterfront district to the west of the city, wandering among stone houses whose doors were locked and lights were off. The Philadelphia skyline shivered in the waters of the Delaware, the streets were empty and poorly lit and a gentle snow slowly covered the pavement, and Antonis Kambanis and his brown suitcase found refuge in the doorway of a shuttered general store where he sank into a sweet sleep, embraced by warm dreams as his eyes closed and his lips turned white and he became one with the snowy landscape—until a sudden, prolonged, violent shaking brought him back to life and his lips were splashed with strong moonshine, a killer grappa that could resurrect even the dead.

Apart from a lingering numbness in his hands and a chill that lay close to his shivering skin, Antonis Kambanis had regained his senses entirely when, thanks to a pantomimed recounting of events and some awkward, jesting gestures toward his new surrounds, he realized he'd woken up in the foyer of a funeral parlor, surrounded by crosses, ebony coffins, and statues of the Virgin Mary, and promptly crossed himself three times and fainted again. When he came to a second time, it was thanks to the ministrations of a middle-aged woman who tenderly sponged his face and gave him salted water to drink, and when he opened his eyes, the warmth and coziness of the atmosphere, the fire burning in a nearby fireplace, and the smell of food cooking all reminded him of his mother, and he began to cry quiet, childish, snotty tears.

He stayed with the family of Tony Mecca for nine days, long enough to regain his strength, sleeping in a small storeroom on the ground floor whose only furnishings were a small sofa and an old hand-crank Berliner gramophone. Right outside the door were stacks of coffins, and the whole ground floor smelled of varnished wood, like a Norwegian autumn, full of birch and pine, rotting leaves and gentle rain, and each night he shut the door tightly and didn't move an inch or sleep a wink for fear that shades, spirits, and voices would haunt his sleep, not to mention thoughts of the death of his mother or his own recent brush with mortality. Three black men had found him slumped in a doorway, discovered his Italian papers and passport in the inside pocket of his suit, and, thinking him already dead, had carried him to Tony Mecca's coffin shop on 4th Street, across from Our Lady of Mt. Carmel in the Italian neighborhood of Central Waterfront, a white two-story house that was both business and home—the funeral parlor was on the ground floor and the family lived on the second. Members of the community would gather downstairs in the evening sneaking nips of drink beside the corpses, supposedly to see them off, and late into the night the place shook with dancing, billiards, and wisecracks. Tony was a natural leader with a quick wit, a joke always at the tip of his tongue, and was always stepping in to help. He would act as volunteer translator, gravedigger, or advisor, he filled out paperwork and applications for the illiterate, buried the poor, showed up in court for his friends, would even give false testimony if the situation called for it, and all because he nursed a secret plan to run for office, to hoist himself up onto the pedestal of posterity— and in fact his reputation and influence in the Italian part of the city was such that whenever newly arrived Italians encountered the question "Where is the White House?" during an exam for a residence permit or coveted green card, they would answer without a second thought, "The white house? That's Tony Mecca's funeral parlor, 4th Street and Division, Camden, New Jersey, United States of America"— and to make sure they were in God's good graces as well, they would add, "across from Our Lady of Mt. Carmel, Full of Grace, Worker of Miracles."

Of course miracles were rare in those days, and if you didn't have Italian blood, let alone if you weren't Catholic, there was no way you were getting through Tony Mecca's front door, you needed the proper credentials to cross that threshold, alive or dead, upright or lying down, and how were those three black men who'd found Antonis freezing in the street to know that Italian papers were carried in the Dodecanese, too, and that he wasn't Catholic but Greek Orthodox, and so when Tony Mecca's henchman Pepito, a bit of a dim bulb, opened the door and started shouting at them, they hastened to present the stamped papers they'd found on the man, and only then did Pepito run to help, pushing the three men aside with Calabrian curses as if they were ominous crows whose dirty talons might defile the body of this noble compatriot who had come, poor sucker, to find his fortune in *mamma mia brutta anche bella America.*

Antonis's luck was quick to turn: Tony Mecca took him under his protection, rented him a room on Bergen Square and promised him a decent wage, as long as he'd do his best to make him proud. At first Tony gave him errands to run, asked him to deliver confidential packages or threatening messages, had him give the occasional thrashing to solve a stubborn mix-up or misunderstanding, and a few months later, once Mecca felt perfectly assured that Antonis not only shared his name—Antonio, Antonis—but was easygoing and trustworthy, he nicknamed him Nondas and brought him fully on board. During the day their gang of four would dress the corpses that crossed their threshold, at night they'd go down into the basement to doctor up their strong, bracing moonshine, and at daybreak, as the sun was just peeking over the horizon, they'd load the carboys into the hearse and Pepito, Sergio, and Antonis would head out on deliveries to a few select customers and friends in high places.

It was on one such morning, as Pepito was hastily unloading with Sergio at the helm and Antonis acting as lookout in the passenger seat, that he first saw her, stepping lightly across Cooper Street, and in the first blush of daylight his eyes were drawn to her blond hair. He noticed the cherry trees in full bloom, the wide, clean streets, the solidly built mansions, and the alabaster sky, and he felt a tightening in his chest, a vise slowly twisting him in its grip, until at last he tore his eyes away to check for danger, and Gina the hearse started up with a hollow squeal and lurched around the next corner. That very night he developed a fever, his nose was stuffy and runny at once, shivers shook his whole body, and a doctor was called, since they'd seen plenty of people laid low by consumption. Dr. Zakolski finally showed up near midnight with his little bag of instruments, and when he'd seen his fill, and of course eaten and drunk, he lit a cigar and confidently declared that the patient would live, the only thing wrong with him was a disinclination to spring, to the cherry trees and magnolias, to the lindens and locusts—in other words, it was a clear case of hay fever. And when Dr. Zakolski finally pushed off sometime past two in the morning, an anxious Nondas crept in to ask the benevolent Mrs. Mecca, who was clearing the table, whether his case was serious and what the prognosis was, and Mrs. Mecca chuckled, shook her head, winked knowingly, and pronounced through a mouthful of crumbs, *"Io sono sigura che ti abbiano fatto il malocchio,"* someone had surely given him the evil eye.

And while it may not have been the evil eye precisely that had brought Nondas to his knees, straining the limits of his endurance with all that sneezing, those red eyes, and a nose that ran like a spigot, he was convinced that his suffering had its roots in female cunning, and if he wanted to break free of those powerful bonds he needed to find that blond beauty again, but the more he searched for her the more despairing he became, the city of Camden was a haystack and he was looking for the one tiny needle that had pricked him, and the more obsessed he became the more Sergio and Pepito teased him and poked fun, pinching and tripping him, cutting jokes, but he didn't give up, he kept his eyes on the prize, defying all of creation as he wiped them, and wiped his streaming nose, even his mouth, as he sneezed— *"achoo! achoo!"*—then again the next moment— "Damn my luck to hell and back, *achoo! achoo!"*

Spring departed, replaced by a brief summer during which his symptoms softened somewhat, then finally one evening toward the end of September he saw her at dusk, she'd stopped on the sidewalk outside his window to shake a bothersome pebble out of her shoe, and Nondas didn't lose an instant, he grabbed his coat and hat and ran into the street to talk to her, but quickly lost his nerve, hesitated for a

moment, and ended up trailing her as she walked—
and the longer he followed the less sure he felt that
it was really her, this girl's hair seemed to have a
reddish tinge he hadn't noticed when he'd first seen
her, though maybe those bronze highlights were
simply a reflection of the rosy twilight. In this un-
certainty he followed her all the way to the Irish
neighborhood of Pine Point—a bit further and Petty
Island would appear in the distance. It was a
strange, uncanny evening that made you believe in
ghosts, pirates, and plundered hearts, there wasn't
another soul in the streets, and Nondas felt spooked
by his own shadow, his footsteps synchronized
with hers and adrenaline flowed through his veins,
she sensed his breathing and his quick, awkward
footfalls behind her and she turned to shout but
before she could make a sound, Nondas grabbed her
and pulled her into his arms, and whatever he did
was done furtively, quietly, and quickly, and was
also immediately forgotten—at least by him—covered and smothered by the thick, oppressive, unre-
lenting dark.

Winter came, the female apparition faded, and
Nondas found his better self again. Work was busy,
orders were multiplying, and they kept taking on
bigger jobs, they couldn't keep up with demand,
couldn't make enough moonshine to supply all
their friends and friends of friends in high places.
They considered starting to smuggle it in from the
frozen lakes of Canada, but Philadelphia was teem-
ing with bigger outfits and ruthless gangs, and
Mecca didn't want to get mixed up in mafias and
messy affairs, his life was in the coffin business and

he was making plenty of money off the underworld as it was, at least for the time being, so he contented himself with the infallible rules of local supply and demand: the longer the city stayed dry, the more valuable his moonshine became—and the thirstier people got for booze and excitement, the better his legal living and side gig too.

Things would have gone on like this, calmly and steadily, if on December 22, 1923, an expensively wrapped, oblong box with a lively red bow hadn't shown up at the Meccas' door. It bore no card, had no sender's or receiver's name, and yet no one found the package suspicious, it was simply set aside and forgotten—after all, it was just a few days until Christmas and perhaps someone wanted to express anonymous gratitude for the Mecca family's generosity, since at some point during the holiday season the family always hosted a gathering of friends and business associates to open the gifts piled under the Christmas tree.

Christmas Eve arrived, the day of the party, and Mrs. Mecca still hadn't found time to buy gifts for all of her guests. There was no one around to help, her daughters were at the seamstress having final alterations made to their dresses for the New Year's ball, Tony had an important meeting with Senator Spacey of the Republican Party in Central Watertown to break bread and barter votes, and she still had to get the house ready and put the stuffed goose in the oven—and meanwhile Sergio impatiently peeled a tub of sweet potatoes, complaining that an overcooked fowl wasn't his idea of a good meal, he'd a thousand times prefer the traditional fried eel with bay leaves and garlic. As the dinner hour neared, Mrs. Mecca grew more and more anxious, and with nowhere else to turn she summoned Pepito and Nondas, who had dressed in their best suits hours ago. She wished them a merry Christmas, praised their devotion and hard work, and pressed ten whole dollars into their hands to go and buy gifts for the rest of the guests on the list—only it was after five, so wherever they went they found stores already closed, and they soon began to despair, Mrs. Mecca had pinned all her hopes on them, they didn't want to disappoint her, but the only shopkeeper they found in the street was old Mr. Stein headed home after closing up shop, a thick bunch of keys hanging from his neck, and when he hesitated, they promised to grease his palm with gold, showing him the crumpled bills in their fists, and Mr. Stein nodded his agreement, it was Christmas Eve, after all, and they wouldn't have much luck finding anyone else out and about, and so the three men hastened together down the street.

The dinner was a great success, the food delicious and filling, the portions generous and accompanied by plenty of red wine—a gift from Lieutenant Rigoletti, who always made sure that whatever illicit goods he confiscated on the job made their way to the homes of his friends—and just before they set out the dessert plates in the candlelight, Tony Mecca put a record on the gramophone of Pasquale Feis singing Sicilian carols accompanied by the eerie, bagpipe-like sounds of the zampogna and gaida, and Mrs. Mecca crossed herself reverently, then called her guests to gather round the tree and open the gleaming presents waiting patiently beneath the shiny baubles and decorations, while Nondas and Pepito looked on, proud as peacocks, their cheeks flushed with wine.

While the guests opened the presents, sometimes trading among themselves according to individual tastes and preferences, Mrs. Mecca plated the velvety tiramisu in the dining room, and when she had finished she joined the others, pulling an oblong, unmarked box out from behind the tree where it had lain forgotten, and as she opened the top she let out a scream: in the box lay a long white robe and a ridiculous pointed cap, the calling card of the Ku Klux Klan.

III

lily:
out of water ...
out of itself
NICK VIRGILIO

When he's worried or upset Basil throws himself into
cooking—the bigger the problem, the more complex
the dish—and as a result Susan has enjoyed the most
inventive delicacies of her life after their biggest
arguments, at moments of personal disappointment
for her husband, and during his intermittent periods
of anxiety over their precarious finances, which
recently seem to be cropping up more and more frequently, or maybe it's just her imagination, a byprod-
uct of suddenly finding everything so overwhelming,
their tentative decisions, the love they share, their
daughter, how every day reminds her of days gone by.
Nine years ago Leto was still a toddler—how old was
she then, two? three?—yes, she'd just turned three
when the fires broke out and the whole city burned
for three days and nights, for three days and nights

stores and houses were looted, the smoke seemed to trap and incite unspoken fears, things had flared up seemingly out of nowhere, at the end of August two police officers beat a Hispanic motorcyclist so badly he ended up in intensive care, the news spread quickly by word of mouth through the projects, blacks and Puerto Ricans grabbed crowbars and torches, formed uneasy alliances in a single night against the threat of white brutality, swore retribution in the name of Horacio Jiménez, and while he fought for his life in the ICU, Susan, fearing the worst, prayed that the doctors would fight tooth and nail, too—and as Horacio's body let its soul go free in the early hours of the morning, Basil wondered what had gone wrong, what had inspired such hatred and rage, what had stirred this flaming tongue that emerged from the depths of night to devour the entire city. In what seemed like a matter of hours, for rent or sale signs sprang up in store windows and outside of houses along the streets of Camden, and within a week property values had hit rock bottom, homes and fortunes were left behind, abandoned forever in a way most of their owners could never have imagined—and there amid the human and residential ruins sat a dazed Susan and Basil and their little Leto.

Susan has been sunk in thought for a while now and hasn't noticed the white-and-orange U-Haul truck into which the few possessions and dated furniture of the family next door are being loaded, or maybe she saw it out the corner of her eye, unconsciously registering the early-morning back and forth between truck and house, and it's dredged up the long-buried realization that life is irrefutably comprised of actions and events, and while the houses we inhabit are built of concrete, glass, brick, and wood, the only thing that's really free and accessible to all is the unmoored muddle of our thoughts, our dreams and aspirations—and Susan is standing stock-still at her five foot ten in the same position, hands at her waist, mouth numb from chewing and swallowing words, and thinking, thinking, she wishes she could stop thinking, and she suddenly spins around and sees Basil behind her, grabs him by the shoulders and shakes as if something momentous and important has just occurred, something that's escaping him, but she still doesn't speak, doesn't tell him about the decision she's made to up and leave—*That's it, enough, fuck it all*—just stands there and silently pleads with him, her crystal blue eyes deepening a shade until they resemble the harbors and coves of the feverish Mediterranean.

"I made pancakes with orange zest," he says, bringing Susan back down to earth. "There's maple syrup on the table, and honey, too," he calls as she hurries past him and rushes up the stairs, because it's 7:15 and Leto is still up to her ears in sheets and blankets, dead set on staying home from school, she's been pretending to be sick since last night, faking a cough, claiming a fever and a sore throat, an earache, a sinus infection, or maybe it's bronchitis, even pneumonia.

Leto rubbed the thermometer between her palms, heated it against the radiator, even snuck a few cloves of garlic out of the kitchen cupboard and tried keeping them under her tongue because she's heard that sometimes does the trick, but the most she could raise her temperature was a fraction of a fraction of a degree, the thermometer stuck stubbornly below the 99-degree mark, and before going out to the car she played her final card, thrashing on the floor, banging her legs, shouting, crying, a toddler-style meltdown as her mother looked on coolly, almost calculating, with those transparent blue eyes that betrayed no emotion at all, so Leto raised her right arm and slammed it hard against the wall. It immediately bruised and swelled up like a balloon, and when Susan grabbed her by that same arm to lift her up Leto let out an inarticulate cry of actual pain, and so now here they are, mother and daughter, sitting in the emergency room at the public hospital as a friendly, white-haired Dr. Malone wraps Leto's arm in plaster, supervised by a sardonically smiling adolescent girl who's just missed a test in American History, and by her mother's scowling Bavarian gaze, which can be traced back through at least three generations of long-buried Suzannes.

The old Plymouth Cricket groans around a curve, Leto is struggling with the broken seat belt on the passenger side, her cast won't fit through the tangled loop of its straps, so Susan hits the brakes, pulls onto the shoulder, puts on her hazards, and sits there waiting for Leto to ask for help. Mother and daughter aren't speaking, each has dug in her heels for her own just and unjust reasons, and as Leto's face flushes with exertion and annoyance Susan turns on the radio and rolls down her window, letting the weak sunlight outline her pale face as the newscaster reports on the presidential race. Reagan's campaign manager is concerned that Carter might secretly negotiate the release of American diplomats being held hostage in Tehran, trying to bring them home before election day so he can win over popular opinion and ride that wave to victory—and then the commentator's voice fades out as the opening riff of Smokie's "Stumblin' In" takes over the airwaves.

Susan leans her head against the door and quietly sings along, she doesn't know all the words but the rhythm and melody are so familiar it's as if she does, and when she turns to look out the passenger-side window, she sees two dark eyes peering in at them, studying mother and daughter curiously, and Leto, sensing a change in the atmosphere, shakes her body and broken arm free of the seat belt, swivels around, and sees Minnie's confusion and shy wave, before the girl quickly lowers her hand, hunches her shoulders, and dips her head as if she's crossed an invisible border, then adjusts her unwieldy, over-stuffed backpack that's far too large and heavy for her small frame, and continues her lonely progression, limping slightly with her left foot because her shoes aren't great and she's already come a long way. A blister is forming on her pinky toe, but she's sure that if she stops now she'll never make it, and she's secretly set a goal—after all, she's always been told she can do anything she sets her heart on—to arrive at her destination, to make it to school even if she's late, because she's done all her homework, every single math problem, and the world rarely gives her any pleasure greater than a teacher's praise.

Susan asks her daughter who the girl with the crooked braids and enormous backpack is, but Leta just shrugs, sticking a mechanical pencil under her cast to scratch at her itchy arm, and her rudeness annoys Susan, who finds herself drawn to something about the strange girl, but she lets it go, she's had a lot on her mind all morning, so she just switches off the radio, starts the car, and turns, the house isn't far, another five minutes or so, and Minnie disappears for the time being from their rectangular field of vision.

Basil Kambanis is standing beside his adopted daughter, writing *Get well soon, comet* in thick permanent marker on her cast, and given that they're not biologically related, it's strange how much she resembles him, that stubborn tuft of hair that keeps falling over her right eye, how every so often she tosses her head or pushes it away with a gesture that seems like the most natural thing in the world. She resembles him too in how easily she can annoy Susan with her superficiality, her constant demands and mulish obstinacy—if the girl or her stepfather set their mind on something, there's no turning back or giving in. Just now Leto shoves the lock of hair out of her eye so she can see what Basil is scrawling on her cast, and he winks at her, wondering out loud, "I mean, how did she just walk into a wall?" and when Leto doesn't answer, Susan says with restrained naturalness, "She went to grab the thermometer as it slipped out from under her tongue, and she hit the wall instead," and Leto snaps, "Just leave me alone, both of you," and storms off, slamming the door behind her—how dare they make fun of her right in front of her eyes, which are now brimming with tears of anger and rage, because she can still taste that garlic, it's still there, it seems to have made a nest for itself under her tongue.

Basil and Susan smile at one another conspiratorially, fine wrinkles like the roots of saplings sprouting at the corners of their eyes and mouths. Susan musses his hair tenderly, Basil takes her hand and kisses it, then wonders out loud, "What are we going to do with that kid?"—a rhetorical question that needs no answer—and Susan admits, "She takes after me," Basil adds, "She doesn't listen," and they both conclude in unison, "It's just a phase," and the words blunt their pain with the recognition that things have to run their course, that time heals all wounds and smooths all the bumps in the road, those tiny fissures that haven't yet become gaps, those vague worries that haven't yet grown to engulf the body, those little white lies and their vague, misleading implications.

A few minutes later Leto clomps down the circular wooden staircase in the duplex dressed for practice, her jacket hanging loosely from her left shoulder since the sleeve won't fit over the cast. "Where do you think you're going?" Susan asks, narrowing her eyes. "To practice," Leto answers drily, and Basil, momentarily at a loss, stammers, "It's probably best to skip practice today, honey." Leto snaps, "Who's taking me? I'm late," and Susan steps toward her daughter angrily, but Leto is feeling defiant, doesn't care about the danger and insists full of nerve and annoyance that she's fine. "Yeah, fit as a fiddle," Susan shoots back, but it's already too late: Leto has swung the door open and is off at a run.

Dashing across the street with her arm in the cast,

Leto looks like a rudderless ship listing slightly to the right, and Susan props one arm against the front door and watches her run off until she disappears entirely. Basil comes and stands behind his wife and rests his palm on her arm, "Why did you let her go?" he asks, and when Susan gently shrugs and says, "What was I supposed to do?" her voice sounds less overbearing, almost apologetic, so much that it scares her, and her back turns and conceals the expression on his face, and the door with its heavy row of locks closes behind them with a lighthearted creak as their momentarily, provisionally ordered lives fit together once more.

Basil's beat-up station wagon pulls into the small parking lot of the Ariadne, it's almost eleven and any minute now lunch customers will start showing up from the handful of office buildings and stores in the area. Sally waves at him through the steamy glass as Veronica serves some free coffee in paper cups printed with amphoras and Parthenons to old Mike and Jason the drunk, neighborhood fixtures, homeless for years, forever moving their cardboard boxes from one empty lot to the next, settling in the doorways of abandoned buildings, the warm entryways of banks and shops, until the rent-a-cops or actual cops get wind of them and send them packing again just to crush their pride, to rub their faces in the fact that they'll never have anywhere to stop and rest their bones, they'll always be wandering from place to place, dragging their boxes and dirty blankets through the streets until the end of time.

Basil enters the diner and greets his girls—neither

of whom will ever see this side of sixty again—then goes over to wrestle with the pile of endlessly proliferating bills eating holes in his pockets, earnings are way down and it's not clear how long he can cover the expenses that keep piling up month after month, and meanwhile Leto is growing, as are her needs, how on earth are they going to find the money to send her to college, a state school would be cheaper, but it's still a hefty sum he isn't sure he'll be able to pay, how is he going to manage it all, Christ, kids grow up so fast, and among the letters and bills he discovers brochures singing the praises of useless products, leaflets inviting him on mythic vacations, pamphlets from the Jehovah's Witnesses, futuristic advertisements for Scientology, Jesus H. Christ, what's happening to the world around him, things are going from bad to worse, rising taxes have brought him to his knees, people are out of work and inflation is spiking upwards—and then the door to the diner opens, the little bell jingles, and the first customers of the day slide onto stools at the counter and order the house special, suicide on a plate: grilled bread stuffed with a thick slice of Spam, two fried eggs, and plenty of melted cheddar, with a side of onion rings that takes up half the plate.

The sunflower oil sizzles over the flame, forming huge golden bubbles that look ready to burst and overflow the deep fryer. Veronica tosses in the frozen onion rings and French fries, breaking them up with a spoon so they'll all turn the proper pinkish yellow color, and Basil's mind wanders as he stares into the deep fryer like he's trying to figure out how many bubbles will fit before they start to spit oil

onto the floor tiles, which over time have accumu-
lated a layer of grime that has seeped into the grout,
or before Sally lays out the silverware and pours
coffee for the customers, whom you can count on
one hand and who rarely order the mouthwatering
gyro or watery tzatziki, or before Susan gets into
her car, which Basil gave her as a first anniversary
gift and which she never liked because of its glaring
cabbagey color and ugly mug, which make it look
like an enormous, repugnant grasshopper.

Minnie turns onto Fremont Avenue and sees her
school rising up before her like a juvenile prison,
filling the whole block with its towering, off-white
walls and huge, red, rusted metal doors, and she
quickens her pace even though her toe is killing her,
any passerby could guess what's wrong from her
limp, but she's so close now to the main entrance on
Stevens Street and she's sure she's made it in time
for her physics class, which she adores—all these
forces working to keep the objects hulking around
her at a safe and balanced distance, the kinetic energy coiled inside her brother's fists, her body a
punching bag, how it sways and responds when the
wind is knocked out of her, the internal oscillation
of a decreasing sine wave that brings her back to her
original inert position, all the things she hates and
loves and feels like she kind of understands, the unpronounceable terms, complex meanings, compli-
cated charts, torques, and forces that overtake her,
centrifugal ghosts that come out late at night and
every so often water her bed with fear.

She opens the door to the classroom and two
dozen pairs of curious eyes turn toward her, and

then the kids break into a cacophony of whispers and giggles at her strange, pitiful, mismatched outfit, and stout Mr. Brown peers at her over his tortoiseshell glasses, waves her over to his desk and asks why she's late, and Minnie doesn't know where to begin, with her brother Pete and her sleepless night, her mother's hysteria, her aching toe, the uneven braids she's just remembered as her fingers fly up again to measure the missing inches, how she couldn't find the right clothes in the drawer, or how she missed the school bus by a matter of seconds— and Mr. Brown, whose patience has been sorely tried and who has no interest in awkward, pointless silences, tells her to sit right down at her desk, she's disturbed his class enough already, she'll have to stay late after school to make up the test she just missed.

The last bell rang a while ago and the classroom is empty of students and sounds, the school busses all pulled away at their usual time, Mr. Brown is correcting papers and Minnie is scratching away at her test with a chewed pencil, apparently she's not as prepared as she thought and her head is starting to buzz, the test is multiple-choice but the choices are traps, every so often a question leaps out at her like a rabbit, she's sure she knows how to answer it, but then the right and wrong answers get tangled up on the page, creating one long smudge with no beginning or end, and Mr. Brown raises his head and looks her way, but his gaze is entirely indifferent, addressed to no one and focused on nothing in particular, then he turns back to his papers as Minnie, distracted, peers down at her muddy sneakers, the soles so worn they look like ballet flats, and she starts to imagine herself twirling in a dance studio, leaping lightly over the parquet, higher and higher, up to the ceiling, only there is no ceiling because there are no ceilings in dreams, and her eyes begin to blur and close, and her eyelids get heavier, heavier and hazier, until her chin hits the desk with a bang and she remembers that the answer to question 17 is B and the letter G is the international symbol for the gravitational constant that at some point brings us all suddenly and abruptly crashing down.

Susan hadn't intended to go out into the streets looking for Leto, but something had stuck in her craw and kept worrying her, and so she drove by the Lions' soccer field as the girls' team was running a final set of sprints before the traditional double lap to end the week, then she stopped at the ice-cream parlor owned by a redhead named Charlton and at the anarchist Friedman's record store, even stopped to ask the elderly Sylvia, an old maid in her 80s who liked for people to call her Miss Janetson, who at the first sign of sunshine dragged a beat-up metal folding chair over to her brother's mini market and sat to rest her arthritic bones—but despite all the searching and asking, Susan never got any closer to an answer, her daughter had simply disappeared again, as she often did when things didn't go her way, and Susan kept wracking her brains trying to figure out where she might have gone, and she was on the verge of giving up, throwing in the towel— only as a mother she had no choice, so she went into autopilot, got in the car again and headed back to the one place she was absolutely sure her daughter wasn't hiding, East Camden Middle School, because she was coming around to the idea that when something disappeared and she went out in search of it, more often than not, despite every logical explanation, it would turn out to have been sitting in plain view all along, right where it belonged.

She parks the car close to the main entrance with the iron gate, where the date of the building's construction, August 1968, has been chiseled in stone and set into the pale cement, and as she steps out of the car she suddenly freezes in the middle of the street, keys dangling from her hand, unable to move forward or back, because she's just remembered the dust bunnies that she swept under the rug again this morning—no matter how often she wipes down the furniture during the day, it mocks her by collecting another thin layer of dust overnight—and she carefully, hesitantly steps forward on tip-toe, not wanting to wake any more memories, and when she reaches the sidewalk she sees a human mass curled into a ball on the curb, gently rubbing its aching toes, and Susan, suddenly dizzy, legs heavy and head light, trips and collapses at Minnie's side, probably because she hasn't eaten all day, she never got the chance and now her stomach is protesting, she's been having these dizzy spells for a month now—could she be?—no, there's no way, on the rare occasions when they have time and are in the mood to make love, they always take precautions, but now she shivers as a chill pierces her bones—could she?—and then all of a sudden she faints, and Minnie finds herself with a strange woman in her arms. Susan is skinny, she has a body type that'll always be thin no matter how much she eats, but Minnie finds herself struggling to keep Susan from toppling onto the cold pavement, and as Susan comes to, her breathing is less sharp and painful, she opens her eyes, already feeling better, trying to rein in the haze by force of will, and Minnie holds her even more tightly as Susan smiles at her and says, "I'm fine, it passed," and she really is fine, it really did pass.

Susan tries to persuade Minnie to get into the car, Centerville isn't far, and though it's after three and during rush hour there's no accounting for traffic, once Susan sets her mind on something there's no going back, but Minnie keeps shaking her head, Louisa made her swear on her mother's life that she'll never get into a stranger's car no matter what, so she shakes her head no, even though her nose is running and she can feel herself getting sick, all that time under a cold drizzling rain in her light jacket, she sneezes and her eyes fill with tears, she doesn't know what to wipe first with her sleeve, and with no good reason left to resist, she lets Susan push her gently into the passenger seat, buckle her in, and turn on the engine, and Minnie sits there quaking with gratitude and fear, not knowing which of the two will win out, and Susan, seeing her shaking, turns the heat on full blast, and the old Plymouth Cricket leaps forward toward the other cars, then slowly inches out into traffic, and Minnie leans her head to one side and nods off as they turn onto Kaighns Avenue—her mouth is open, leaking saliva and soft little snores. Susan takes a deep breath, it's strange how eleven whole years of marriage can squeeze their way into a traffic jam like this. Through the closed car window Susan sees an old woman in a gray sedan with narrow wrists, a cigarette dangling from her lips, and knows that'll be her in a few years, sees a dark-haired man who reminds her of her first awkward kiss in a crumbling treehouse on her grandfather's farm, sees a plump young woman dozing at the wheel while the light is red, and in the white Chevrolet in front of her a sad-looking girl with a tight ponytail keeps twisting her whole body around to stare at her though the rear window as Susan's gaze wavers in place and time, before falling with a resigned thud on Minnie's childish face as the girl slowly opens her eyes and stretches her arms, returning Susan to the impatient present, the always urgent and insistent now.

Susan waits in the car to make sure the girl can get inside as Minnie knocks on the front door for Louisa to open, in her haste that morning she forgot her keys on the kitchen counter, but the door doesn't open and Minnie keeps knocking with no response, so Susan locks the car, walks over to the girl and asks if there's a back door or a window that might be open, and Minnie leads her around the side of the house, where the kitchen window looks sidelong onto the street, and Susan cups her hands and rests them against the glass to banish the glare as Minnie stands on tiptoe to peek in, only she's too short by a good ten inches and Susan feels the chilly November wind slipping under her blouse, a wind that's picking up, blowing down from Montreal and the distant Arctic beyond, a wind that freezes everything except time.

IV

There is something in staying close to men and women and
*   looking on them, and in the contact and odor of them,*
*   that pleases the soul well,*
All things please the soul, but these please the soul well.
WALT WHITMAN

Mrs. Mecca is flustered, she cut her thumb and burned the porcini risotto and now the blood won't stop, it's dripping all over her freshly mopped floor, another tiny drop every second, and there's no one else at home. Tony and his crew are at a funeral and her daughters are at their Wednesday choral practice, and all kinds of thoughts are spinning through her head, her husband's stubborn insistence on joining the Republican ticket and running for office, her daughters growing up and starting to have lives of their own. The other day she caught Anna-Maria smoking in secret and the girl had the nerve to slam the door in her face, and as for Costanza, she's so serious and reserved that Mrs. Mecca is terrified she might end up an old maid—what she needs is a little spark to light her up. But above all, she's plagued by the thought of the butchered, plucked chicken she found this morning right out in the open, sunning itself in her vegetable patch, legs splayed, a message scrawled on its chest in black permanent marker: *Dago go home.*

She crossed herself three times in a row, put the bird in a black plastic bag, and went across the street to find the Catholic priest and ask his opinion and advice. Her husband just won't listen to reason, not even when she gave him a piece of her mind after that fiasco at Christmas, what business did he have getting mixed up in politics, and the whole moonshine madness had gone too far, didn't they earn plenty as it was from dolling up corpses, weren't they making enough money already off of other people's pain, she'd had it up to here with his endless ambition, when she met him he'd been picking apples in Massachusetts, apples and chestnuts on the farms around Tyngsborough, he didn't have two nickels to rub together, all he could offer was love and silk ribbons, but she fell for him because he was a straight shooter, you could build an entire life on his broad shoulders—only now that solid structure was listing to one side like the leaning tower of Pisa and she wasn't about to let him do as he pleased without putting up a good fight, she knew Mecca needed a bit of a scare and was hoping the heavens would throw up some temporary obstacle until she could figure out her next move, and so she headed over to the church across the way to spill the whole story, except for the bits that might have landed them straight in the county jail, and as evidence of her personal trials and tribulations she brought along the black bag containing the ominous, ritually disemboweled fowl.

The aged Reverend Christopher Leone, with his pot belly and graying goatee, had been eating a quick lunch at the altar, beleaguered and exhausted by his flock's constant complaints and rivalries regarding the raising of funds for a new bell tower, why on earth were they so keen on holding concerts and raffles in the dead of winter, he wondered, chewing the slightly stale bread as crumbs fell onto the altar like tiny flecks of his own inconsequence and decline, and how were they going to come up with seventy-five thousand dollars, how many concerts and dances did he have to endure in the name of the Lord, who, according to his parishioners, wanted nothing more than the resounding peal of a new church bell to bring the ringing tones of mortal supplication to His all-hearing ear—so when Mrs. Mecca had crossed the nave and slipped up beside him, Reverend Leone jumped, startled, and a bit of his sandwich went down the wrong pipe as another shower of crumbs rained down from his cassock to the altar, much to Mrs. Mecca's delight: she now had a certain indisputable, if fleeting, advantage, thanks to the omnipresent, all-pervasive Catholic sense of guilt, since she was quite certain that our Lord had no desire for anyone to be spraying stale crumbs all over his church.

As Reverend Leone saw it, all kinds of strange things had been happening in his parish over the past few weeks, as if someone was maliciously clanging some internal bell at odd and uncertain hours, and no matter how hard he tried, he was no closer to solving the mystery. How was he to explain the Protestant Pastor Moore's invitation to discuss a delicate and confidential personal matter, or the hasty knock at the church door two days ago that resulted in no visible presence, or the widow Monica Sclavi's unexpected invitation to a tête-à-tête dinner to discuss an issue that indirectly affected him, or perhaps she'd said directly—his memory was a sponge that was now alarmingly oversaturated with trivial information about equally trivial meetings and events—and it all smelled fishy to him, the devil had many legs, not to mention cuckold's horns, and the reverend, who knew plenty about underhand tricks from his childhood years in Manduria, in the province of Taranto, was keeping his mouth shut and his eyes peeled until he could figure out what demon was pulling the strings of what wicked and precarious plan, and therefore he showed little excitement as he greeted Mrs. Mecca with a wary smile.

"Satan worshippers," no doubt about it, Reverend Leone declared as he examined the plucked fowl bearing the racist slogan, and then he asked Mrs. Mecca if she remembered having seen anything else strange or foreboding, anything out of the ordinary, and Mrs. Mecca lowered her eyes and swallowed her words, no, nothing worth mentioning, because at Christmas her husband had told her that the Ku Klux Klan robe wasn't just an unseasonable Carnival farce, no, some political rival had spread the rumor on the Irish side of town that Mecca and his crew were selling moonshine in Little Italy, capturing profits that could have been theirs, not much, but also not nothing, and the Irish needed to settle the issue as quickly as possible, to send a message, some kind of threat, and for a price Bobby O'Ryan, son of a Protestant father and Catholic mother, had tipped off the Puritan Anglo-Saxon old guard, who saw their values tottering, their youth bewitched by licentious dancing, losing their heads to drugs and spiked drinks, and so those two opposing factions, the Irish and English, decided to join forces and act as one. And if the warning wasn't heeded, they had other, more imaginative means at their disposal that experience had shown were unquestionably effective.

Before Mrs. Mecca could admit it was useless to try and quell her husband's electoral aspirations, Reverend Leone placed a phone call to Lieutenant Rigoletti about this worrisome affair, which would spread panic through the small community if word got out, for in Mrs. Mecca's flushed face he saw his own fears, responsibilities, and oversight, while Mrs. Mecca, who had a great deal on her tormented mind, saw in the church's stained glass the shadow of Tony Mecca rising up like a vengeful god, raising his index finger sternly to accuse her of making a mess of things once again, of getting them into a new muddle, yet another scrape, turning things upside-down, *sottosopra*, and while a jumble of dishes and flavors might come together nicely in her kitchen, in his own life, and certainly in an electoral race, every step needed to be planned, carefully considered, calculated many times in many ways, sketched out and settled on in advance.

The second appalling fowl made its appearance in the living room the following night, came soaring through the window that looked onto the yard while Mrs. Mecca was trying to butter her husband up enough to tell him what had transpired the previous day, she'd made the priest and police officer promise not to say a word until she could make her case to her husband and admit that she'd gone and gotten others mixed up in their family affairs, but while she was still laying the groundwork for her confession, a deafening crack sent them flying to the floor, and when they lifted their heads to see what had befallen them out of the blue, they saw a shattered windowpane and the beady eyes of a well-fed rooster, and Mrs. Mecca, overwhelmed by so much drama in the space of a few days, clamped a hand over her mouth and ran straight for the kitchen, and as she shook with overpowering sobs, it crossed her mind that it would be a long time before she would eat chicken cacciatore again, and her tears broke like a summer storm, raining down on the counter and floor.

Mecca called his crew to a meeting that same night on the ground floor beside the coffins and carboys of grappa waiting to be delivered. Lieutenant Rigoletti squirmed in his seat the entire time, keeping his mouth tightly sealed, something in this whole business made him uneasy, he felt as if his entire career were resting on this night, it would be a risky and desperate act for them to corner Senator Spacey and talk to him straight, and it probably wouldn't get them anywhere anyhow, since his supporters were primarily old guard Anglo-Saxons who were wary of change, while to take on the Irish block and its economic interests, which extended over the entire Northeast, would be sheer suicide—they had to act cleverly and quietly, to make a deal that might drastically reduce their profits and his kickbacks but would bring about the reconciliation necessary for them all to coexist, each earning a part of the profits according to their connections, resources, and abilities in the turfs and speakeasies scattered across the city and its suburbs.

And yet here was Tony Mecca talking about increasing profits and expanding operations into neighboring Philadelphia to fund his campaign, they should strike while the iron was hot, in a few months the great Benjamin Franklin Bridge would be open for business, uniting the bustling metropolis of Philadelphia with its promising, rapidly developing sister city of Camden—they were only two miles apart, and those two miles had the potential to make fortunes overnight, there was already talk of a second Brooklyn, a grand new Camden that would emerge as the city ceased to be a mere commercial and residential satellite of the more densely populated Philadelphia, there were plans in the works for major investment and development, costly construction, beautiful boulevards and well-tended streets, parks and luxury hotels.

The hour grew late, it was nearly daybreak and no decision had been made nor conclusions drawn—they just kept clucking like hens among the caskets, rehashing the same arguments, until Nondas took the floor and proposed the obvious: they should join forces with the Irish, sell them grappa at wholesale prices and let the bogtrotters do the legwork of distributing it, no one would lose out with that kind of arrangement, the profit margins were plenty big for them to split down the middle, not to mention all the time and trouble they'd save, in fact since they wouldn't be riding around all day in a hearse full of booze they could easily increase production, so their profits might even—and before he finished his phrase, Tony Mecca's eyes started flashing, because, yes, *ma che cazzo*, the Greek was right, how had he not thought of it himself, he'd send a messenger that very day to request a secret meeting, it was time for them to act together, as brothers, for the good of Camden and the new era that was dawning.

A meeting was arranged on neutral ground, in the back room of a flower shop in Dudley, East Camden, where a card game started up each evening and dice skittered over the floor, punctuating the sound of bets and Greek laments, and as the hours wore on a badly maintained gramophone would start scratching out rembetika and smyrneika at top volume, the voice of Marika Papagika sang *aman aman* and a dozen grizzled gamblers accompanied her under their breath through the smoke and their own groans of disappointment, and every so often you heard players' breath and hearts stop, the rhythm and beat replaced by the rattling of the dice, which stole joy and left longing in its place.

Stamoulas was five and a half feet tall on a good day and not much to look at, with a nasty scar on his neck from a heck of a fall at a building site where he'd slipped from the scaffolding of a half-constructed mansion and taken a nose dive from thirty feet up, it was a miracle he'd survived, and every Sunday, rain or shine, he went to Philadelphia to light a candle at

St. George's, it was his promise to the Lord, on the condition that He would never let Stamoulas fall like that again, and as long as things stayed on the up and up he kept his word, and thank heavens he made a decent living off the flower shop, which of course he supplemented with these off-the-books earnings as an underground craps and cards establishment. The idea had come to him one day on the construction site, where the Poles and Italians often bet their wages at dice, stretching a threadbare blanket over the ground and smoothing out the wrinkles so the dice would roll gently and straight, and since management had no patience for betting, Stamoulas often acted as lookout to shield the group from prying eyes, and if any curious bastard came nosing around he would hammer on the joints to signal to the others that danger was lurking nearby, and they would pull up the blanket with the dice inside and pretend to be just passing by, whistling some jaunty tune.

The Greek let them use the back room by the emergency exit that opened onto the alleyway, a small room just big enough for a round table and five rickety chairs, with bad lighting and walls yellow with damp and grime. Tony and Big Ray, the boss of northwest Camden, sat at the table, with Rigoletti and Bobby O'Ryan as witnesses and intermediaries, while Neil, Big Ray's stooge, stood at attention behind him and Nondas kept a lookout by the door in case any stray cops wandered that way. One chair sat empty over to the side, and just as they were signaling to one another that they might as well begin, Reverend Leone stumbled in, out of breath, looked them all one by one in the eye, then sat down, sighing and shaking his head, and said "Forgive us, oh Lord, your sinners," and everyone immediately lowered their eyes—after all, all of them except Nondas were Catholic, and so ruled by a shared religious sentiment and fear of divine punishment, even those who had never set foot in a church or chapel, such as Neil, who'd considered priests bad luck ever since he was a kid and his folks were mowed down in a church in Belfast, a spray of bullets to the jugular their punishment for being founding members of Sinn Féin, and Reverend Leone, to make his presence even more deeply felt, crossed himself three slow and dramatic times as he intoned the words "Peace be upon my children," implicitly inviting the gathered group to come to some diplomatic and mutually advantageous understanding.

The biggest sticking point in the negotiations was the percentages: the Irish balked at the idea of a fifty-fifty split, they'd be using their hard-earned network on land and sea, their connections, their trucks and boats, so those pasta-slurping dagos would have to be flexible with their demands, whereas Tony thought the sixty-five–thirty-five the micks were demanding was sheer banditry and dug in his heels at fifty-five–forty-five. Big Ray just tapped his fingers rhythmically and impatiently on the table—and then, seeing that the conversation was going nowhere fast, he stood, picked up his hat, and started to walk off, as Neil aimed two fingers first at Tony then at Nondas, pulling an imaginary trigger, and then followed his boss out of the room, leaving the two men behind struggling to keep their cool, suddenly feeling like the walking dead. Sure, this time they'd live, but it was anyone's guess for how long—which is to say, something had to be done, and quick.

So Tony sent Nondas scurrying after them to accept the deal—"Fuck it, what do we have to lose?"—only now the terms had changed, to seventy-five–twenty-five, and they'd better not keep anyone waiting, Big Ray had bigger pokers in the fire, and Nondas came creeping back in like a wet cat, and that night they sat silently in the Greek's shop, drinking tsipouro and retsina and smoking hand-rolled cigarettes and, with the exception of Reverend Leone, all getting drunk as skunks over the battle and indeed the war they'd just lost. Tony wasn't the mafia type, he was a goddamned skittish immigrant with a coffin business who made moonshine on the side, helped his neighbor as much as he could, and had grand aspirations of becoming mayor, of shaking off once and for all the stigma and fear of poverty he'd been carrying around since he was a kid running wild in the streets of Empoli.

Then, just when everyone seemed to be getting used to the new reality, for better or worse, Reverend Leone rose to his feet and launched into a speech, informing them that he had dined the night before with the widow Monica Sclavi, who intended to remarry and move to Miami. "So what?" Tony barked, annoyed, but the priest plowed on with his story, her fiancé was a Protestant whose family line could be traced generations back to the coastal village of Aberlady on the frozen shores of Scotland—and as the reverend spoke, Lieutenant Rigoletti couldn't suppress a yawn as he thought about the many hours of sleep he'd lost and how much he was dreading the plodding morning patrol that awaited him very shortly on the streets of Centerville, but the reverend simply took out a cigarette, lit it, and crossed his arms as if in spartan and humble prayer, then struck them all with a bolt of lightning, "She's marrying Joseph MacMillan in three months and Pastor Moore and I will be performing the ceremony together," he blurted, then clamped his mouth shut, smothering his laughter and cigarette smoke between teeth and tongue.

The news dropped on them like a bomb. What business did Monica Sclavi, former wife of their dearly departed brother in arms, Pietro Sclavi, have with the despicable Joseph MacMillan, why on earth would she be spending time with him at all, it was inconceivable, Pietro and Joseph had been sworn enemies since their youth, rumor even had it that the Scotsman MacMillan was the leader of the local chapter of the Ku Klux Klan and went down south every so often for his marching orders, and whether or not it was true, MacMillan certainly had it in not just for blacks but for Catholics, Commies, and Jews, his boys were now infiltrating the fire department and the police force, licking boots and starting brawls. Only that wasn't the whole story, as the widow Sclavi had revealed to Reverend Leone during the recent private dinner she had served him by tremulous candlelight: Joseph MacMillan and Pietro Sclavi had in fact been more than enemies, they'd been bitter arch-friends and occasional lovers, and Monica Sclavi made the reverend kiss a cross and promise to take that secret with him to the grave, and he had acquiesced, because he saw in her succulent lips the embodiment of sin itself, the devil playfully swishing his tail, why on earth were people always getting him mixed up in their loves and lusts, "Damn it all, anyhow," he said as he blew his nose noisily into his handkerchief, let God be the one to judge his obligingness, his good intentions, and the tidy sum the widow and her fiancé had promised to contribute toward the construction of the new bell tower in exchange for officiating at this heterodox wedding.

At the end of the day, though, Reverend Leone wasn't the only one with a hidden interest in the wedding going off without a hitch. Tony Mecca was eager to cozy up to the white knights and grand magis so they would stop sending him slaughtered fowl and he could enter the electoral season sound and unscathed, perhaps with a certain advantage, and he might even be able to strike a better deal with the Irish; while Lieutenant Rigoletti would surely profit in various ways from turning a blind eye and writing off the misdemeanors of all involved; and as for the groom, Joseph MacMillan, in addition to the love blossoming late in life between him and the widow and former beauty Monica Sclavi, the marriage would make him even richer, though his personal fortune was the already quite tidy sum of seven hundred thousand dollars and change, the core of which he had supposedly earned by his own sweat and toil, then invested in giddily climbing stocks and fleet-footed trains that crisscrossed the industrially developing states of the eastern seaboard.

The wedding took place on July 4, 1926, a day of commemoration and celebration, not only because it was Independence Day, preparations for which had swathed the city in garlands and flags, but also because that same historic day had been chosen for the ribbon-cutting ceremony at the great Benjamin Franklin Bridge, a nearly two-mile span over the Delaware River uniting Camden and Philadelphia, a bridge that residents of the city would now be setting foot on for the very first time. The wedding was a boisterous, jovial affair full of pomp and banter at Our Lady of Mt. Carmel, under the harsh, merciless eye of Senator Spacey, who waited in vain for something to spark a change in the atmosphere, for the blood to rise and men to start pulling out knives, because a thing like this had never happened before in their small city, the descendants of British colonizers rubbing shoulders with Italian economic migrants, first at a wedding and then crossing a dazzling new bridge side by side and arm in arm, a new day seemed to be dawning in Camden, a bright, shiny new day, as gleaming church bells sang their praise over the land, in all directions, to be heard by all.

And as the wedding guests and curious crowds gazed on the first fireworks to shatter the rapidly darkening sky, Antonis Kambanis, also known as Nondas, reached the far end of the bridge and set foot in Philadelphia, and he felt a tightening in his chest, standing there on an unstable border whose lines had the tendency to shift, fluctuating in a way he found oppressive, and from that side of the river Camden seemed ugly to him, a kind of man-child, it was a thousand times better to look out over the beautiful skyline of Philadelphia with its tall buildings and unfamiliar prospects—and standing here on the opposite side, it was impossible for him to imagine his life otherwise, because this was the life he was living, with its joys and its sorrows, and that knowledge tormented him, the pain smothered him, as the wedding guests huddled together for their final commemorative photographs before night fell—and as he was staring at his dusty shoes with the worn soles, he raised his eyes and saw her, a skinny angry redhead with a smattering of freckles across her nose and cheekbones who strode over to him and stood there bolt upright, eyes flinty and fists clenched, and then out of the blue, with no warning at all, she let out a howl and rushed at him full force, and the crowd and guests froze for an instant, an instant that lasted no longer than the click of a Rolleiflex camera.

V

over the city
the shadow of the falcon
follows the pigeon
NICK VIRGILIO

Susan Miller Kambanis is washing the dishes that
have piled up in the sink, scrubbing dried cereal off
ceramic bowls and coffee stains off the lips of mugs,
the dishwasher is on the fritz again, and the freezer,
too, it's as if household appliances share some
strange code of honor and all decide together when to
act up or suddenly go on strike, or maybe it's just a
small reminder of the ghost of decline that haunts all
our habits, conveniences, and ways of taking care,
the delusion that the silver will always be shiny, the
linens blindingly white, the clothes in the closet fragrant and ironed—and as she's thinking all this, a
grain of dust or some bit of fuzz or a tiny black gnat,
who knows, flies into Susan's eye and clouds her
vision and judgment, blurs those eyes that are trying
so hard to focus on what's in front of them, nothing

more or less than a dozen dirty dishes that didn't get cleaned yesterday or the day before, because the sadness she feels these days is old and familiar, it's carried her to landscapes and seas that have existed since the beginning of time, and she's often tried to close the door on it in the past, but the sadness always sneaks back in, finds a chink in the armor, and now it's slipped in through the cracks and drenched the house in a waning, late-afternoon light. Susan and Basil aren't speaking, they haven't said a word to one another in two days, though who's even counting, and she's entirely sure that a shapeless baby is once again making urgent demands on her body, and meanwhile Leto is all sulking and back talk, and, rather than supporting Susan, her husband simply can't understand what crazy idea came over her, why she decided to bring an abandoned child into their home, of all things, as if what they really need is another mouth to feed, and for the past two days Minnie has been holed up in Leto's room, she won't come out, won't even eat, just sits there waiting for darkness to fall so she can stare out the window at the stars, because somewhere up there her mother Louisa must be settling into her new life-after-life, and tonight Minnie apologizes yet again, begs her mother to forgive her for disobeying, for breaking her promise, she's sorry, so sorry, she swears she didn't mean to, she was so cold, otherwise she would never have gotten into a stranger's car.

And as Minnie is lying in bed striking up a conversation with God who lives up there in the sky, the doorknob turns and Leto comes in moping and frowning, with her arm in a cast, asking how long

Minnie intends to stay in her room, how much longer she's going to inconvenience them all with her presence, before settling down onto the bed like it's a throne, like it's *her* throne—it *is* her bed, after all—and she sits there across from Minnie who's still staring up at the sky and ostentatiously ignoring her; and Leto, not to be outdone by the silent treatment, insists, no, she really wants to know why she's still sleeping on the sofa in the living room, how much longer before she can relax and kick back in her own room again, surrounded by walls that have kept her company since she was a kid, the huge poster of Karl-Heinz Rummenigge and the smaller one of dreamy Matt Dillon, though of course the sofa does have one undeniable advantage, the television she can flip to whatever channel she wants after everyone else is in bed, to watch shows she's never been allowed to see before, like *Kojak*, about the tough New York detective with a weakness for lollipops and hard-hitting interrogations, played by Telly Savalas, who her grandfather actually knew in real life, and *Barnaby Jones*, about a retired detective and his beautiful, widowed daughter-in-law, Betty Jones, who join forces to solve the murder of Hal Jones, their respective son and husband, and Leto is convinced there's a brilliant, capable detective hiding inside of her, full of rage and a sharp gaze, able to find ingenious solutions at the drop of a hat and show everyone who she really is, and as she considers her current problems, which are in definite need of some quick solutions, she shoves Minnie, who still doesn't make a sound, then gives her a shake and offers a truce until further notice—at least until CBS has finished its midnight reruns of the third season with the grizzled, tough-as-nails, swoon-worthy Kojak.

Leto flounces back out of her room, and just as she's jerking the door closed behind her, Basil comes into the house sunk in thought, troubled by the rusty hinges that creak every time anyone opens the front door, the gutters full of fallen leaves, the exterior that needs at least two coats of paint, these odd jobs have been piling up for months, he has the bad habit of letting them fester until they're actually urgent, can't be put off any longer, and finally pull him out of the stoic lethargy that's had him saying, one more day, tomorrow, I'll do it tomorrow—and when he looks up, his eyes meet Leto's entirely reasonable puzzlement, because these thoughts have been playing across his face, and for the first time he feels incapable of hiding from anything or anyone, he can't even hide his disgust for the person he's slowly become, what happened to all those years and dreams, who snuck up and stole the insouciance of his youth, and who is this tall blond girl who calls him dad yet looks so unlike him—there's another thing he never managed, to create life from his life, to give his seed a chance to sprout, not just sow it in condoms and on sheets, and his failure squeezes him like some form-fitting piece of clothing, a too-tight undershirt reminding him of the extra pounds bunched at his waistline, hanging around his middle like a life preserver there to save him from sea swells and squalls, and Basil, who has always loved to swim, particularly the backstroke, remembers his father teaching him how to float on his back during the summer of 1946 in Tampa, Florida, and talking to him for the first and last time about his grief-stricken island with the ashen rocks and smattering of white houses, the sleeping volcano that bubbled at night, and their mountain village, Emporios, riding the sunset's spine—and when they started home that evening on I-95 in their rented sedan, Antonis Kambanis didn't say a word, a deep mourning had sealed his mouth, and for the whole ride home he gripped the steering wheel and grieved for the body of his mother who had died in his absence, with no son to cry at her funeral, and grieved for his own body, too, which— *ashes to ashes and dust to dust*—would one day feed this strange and inhospitable land.

Basil Kambanis stops short in the kitchen doorway and looks at Susan, bent over the sink with her back to him, and her nape seems like an extension of those arms that never rest, as if they've been programmed to perpetual motion since the dawn of time, one always following the other so as not to disturb whatever keeps them tied together, and Basil rests the weight of his body against the doorframe, unsure whether to cross the invisible line that's lain between them for the past two days, and as he ponders his next move—forward or back?—a fragile porcelain plate slips from her hand and shatters loudly in the sink, and their shared surprise over this unexpected accident has something to do with a deep-seated, invisible enemy that cares nothing for his fear or her stubbornness, her sadness or his tendency to procrastinate, because disaster always comes uninvited, it gnaws away at the beams like woodworm, and though the house is still standing around them, the wear and tear has gotten into their hearts, their joy and excitement have dried up, and Basil Kambanis turns on his heel, walks out through the back door, and sits down on the steps of the wooden porch.

Basil's thoughts are as forking and unkempt as the bare branches of the red mulberry tree that shades the house, it's been two months since he got an offer to sell the diner at a bargain price, someone wants to knock it down and open a parking lot for the smattering of two-bit legal and accounting offices, it's not much money, but it's not nothing either, and it's certainly not an unreasonable offer, they can start over in a new, more amenable place, he's not too old for a fresh start, he's only forty-three, still fairly young, even if he's been working since he was sixteen, he might have led a life full of bad decisions so far, but maybe it's time for things to balance themselves out, he can pay off their debts, sell the house for whatever it'll get, it'll be worth it just to be free of the trouble and worry of watching the place lose value year after year—and yet something ties him to this city, he's never known any other, hasn't travelled much, is wary of change, how is it possible for a person to rebuild themselves from the ground up, and, of course, there's their new dark-skinned housemate with her piercing eyes and uneven braids, the girl frightens him, he's afraid of human pain, of abandonment and poverty, how long will it take for welfare services to find her a new home and family, he's heard of cases that take months, even years, what was his wife thinking, going down to the offices and signing the papers, even taking care of the funeral arrangements, she didn't even ask his opinion, and now there's this ghost of a child with her intense, bottomless dark eyes living in his house, and her sorrow makes them all fall quiet and listen to the pockets of emptiness inside themselves—he'll sell the diner, there's no sense fighting the bills and debts that keep piling up day after day, and what worries him the most, it's funny, really, is how he'll tell his girls, Sally and Veronica, who haven't set a dime aside for their retirement, and that solid tree is his only support, the red mulberry with his initials carved in the bark, *B.K*, his own small secret snippet of immortality, and he knows that long after he's ceased to exist, that ancient tree will carry the mark of his hand, two letters and a dot in the middle, that tiny dot containing the whole of his family tree.

Susan sits and eats alone on a stool at the kitchen counter, eyes fixed on the wall, as Leto clumsily chews a slice of pizza in front of the television where a basketball game is playing, and even though she finds the sport boring—it's so incredibly predictable, the best team always wins—she's magnetized by the sight of Magic Johnson, the Lakers' smiling giant, with his clever face and sleight-of-hand passes, and Basil comes and stands next to her, pretending to watch the game, the man-to-man defense on the court, the rough blocking, the weak side trying to screen, an unsuccessful spin move, a stolen pass, and a breakaway that ends in both a basket and a foul, and he's standing there wanting to say something, even some pointless comment that will mean only what it means, about tomorrow's forecast of blustery weather, gusts from the northwest, or the phone bill that's due in two days, the price of gas up to a dollar fifteen, the new national speed limit of 55 miles an hour, intended to help drivers across the country get better mileage during the oil crisis, how inflation is eating away at the two thousand dollars or so he's got in his bank account, and he knows his breath is thick and sour from not eating, he'd like to put a bite or two in his mouth, it'd be easier than just pronouncing the self-evident truth, admitting to his daughter that he's not feeling so well, and besides, words, like thoughts, can't be eaten, won't make a body full, don't nourish, and are themselves nourished only by self-delusions—and as he hesitates for a moment about what to say or do, Magic Johnson scores with a jump shot that seems to defy gravity, and Basil swoops down and masterfully grabs the very last bite off of Leto's plate, the bite she's been saving, a bite of fluffy, crunchy crust, because he's finally ready to face his hunger, his daughter's shouts of rage, and his wife's silence, a silence that creeps across the floor, tiptoes along the counter, staggers through the depths of the kitchen.

Susan is preparing a tray for Minnie, a bowl of vegetable soup, a slice of buttered bread, a square of dark chocolate in the corner for dessert, and Basil opens the fridge and faces his options head-on, and though he doesn't particularly feel like carbs, his hands move on autopilot, pulling out the ingredients for pesto, tossing spaghetti into the boiling water, and the blue flame leaping out of the gas burner hypnotizes him as the blender chops the ingredients into tiny identical pieces and the fresh basil finally smothers the rancid taste that's been lingering in his mouth for days from too many French fries at the diner and the stream of cigarettes he smokes on the sly in the parking lot or on the back porch, and as he shoves a few hurried bites into his mouth, Susan comes back into the kitchen and sends a bolt of lightning flying at him, "If there's one thing I can't stand, it's sulking, and you know it," and he's flooded by a quiet sense of grievance, his guts feel like a tangled ball of yarn, the food won't go down, it gets stuck midway, hovering in his gullet, trying to decide whether to climb back up or slide down—and he makes up his mind to swallow this insult, too, pushes back his plate, grips his fork tightly in his raised fist, and announces his decision to sell the diner and the house, which are his by right and happen also to be legally in his name.

The baby is his, too, by right, at least in part—half of it by weight, a lung, a kidney, half a gallbladder,, half a heart—and as Susan mulls it all over, yesterday's positive pregnancy test in the bathroom floats back up to her mind, the dark-brown ring in the center of a reddish-gold circle shaped by three drops of urine, and she shifts her weight forward onto the balls of her feet as if testing her arches to see if they have the strength and endurance needed for this marathon through a wild forest where the deepest human instincts lie in wait, with claws instead of faces, hands that grab and grasp and stuff their crooked, poison-dripping mouths, and as she silently counts the days and months, estimating with a mother's instinct the size of the fetus inside her, no more than seven or eight inches, a confused, tangled skein of first, hesitant kicks, the tight hugs of childhood, the pangs of adolescence, and grown-up love, none of which it will ever know, because what Susan wants more than anything is to protect it from this cruel, inhuman world, and from all her own mistakes, and her mind's eye scans a fantastical parade of all her minor defeats and majors disappointments, as if she's reliving the first light drizzle that became a crushing rain at Woodstock, 1969, and she wonders yet again how so much love and hope, so many dreams, could have ended up wallowing in the muck and mud of circumstance.

The Plymouth Cricket slows, Susan can barely see the road in front of her, it's been raining since morning and the roads are badly paved, asphalt threaded with puddles of muddy water, the windshield wipers swish, streetlights blink from red to green, and as she nears her destination, Cherry Hill takes shape before her, a suburb full of well-heeled third-generation immigrants, Poles and Italians, Jews and Greeks, living proof of the American Dream, a neighborhood boasting wide streets, spacious, middle-class, cookie-cutter homes with grassy lawns, basketball and tennis courts, private clubs and public pools, perks and amenities befitting doctors and lawyers, big-time accountants, economists who claim to have foreseen the oil crisis, businesspeople who trade futures and derivatives on the stock market, tenured professors who dream of all-expenses-paid trips to conferences in distant cities, scientists and engineers with visions of a bright, globalized future and a communications revolution that will transform all of humanity, and in the cramped Plymouth, Susan feels the seat belt tight against her belly—today when she weighed herself she discovered she's gained twelve pounds—her breasts and cheeks are strangely swollen, and as she swerves to avoid a pothole in the road she catches sight of the Amazon Health Center, a small, self-managed clinic built brick by brick by a group of feminists who hired doctors and nurses with democratic ideals to ensure, in spite of the times and conservative opposition, the inalienable right to self-determination, which is to say the right to abortion, and as Susan enters the clinic her gaze falls first on a pile of pamphlets full of useless statistics and boring information, and then on the brown-haired receptionist sitting behind the desk in a sleeveless denim shirt, with short, shiny, spiky hair and gorgeous tattoos on her arms and neck.

In the procedure room Dr. Ulven slowly explains what's about to happen and, with a performative flair, how they'll slowly dilate her cervix and slide in a special little vacuum, which makes Susan think of the Hoover tucked behind the kitchen door that she uses to clean the house, and how he'll remove the embryo and its surrounding membranes from her uterus, then go back in with a tool called a curette, a kind of tiny scraper, to check for any remnants of embryonic tissue, and again she pictures the scraper they used to clean the windows when they first moved into their house, the entire procedure will take only a few minutes and she'll be sedated the whole time, protected from pain, free even of the weight that keeps her pinned to the exam chair, and when she wakes up from the anesthesia they'll keep her for observation for another few hours and then call her a taxi, she shouldn't have told her husband he didn't need to come, what was she thinking, that she would pop right back up and hop in the car and head for home a few pounds lighter? No, there's a necessary order to things, the doctor declares, and the nurse nods her head in agreement as she slips the needle for the anesthetic into Susan's vein, and now there's no going back, no space for second or third thoughts, she'll have to tell herself afterward that she did the right thing, because now her mouth is going numb, her hands seem to be sinking, weighty and soggy, and her eyes grow heavy, too, diving into a dark blue that slowly becomes a colorless abyss.

"It was a boy," the nurse Alicia says, full of bitter sadness, as soon as Susan comes to. Alicia has given birth three times but only to girls, and all her other pregnancies have been girls as well, and since the poor woman didn't want any more girls, when she learned the sex she aborted them, just as Susan had aborted her unwanted baby today, and when Alicia turned forty she finally admitted to herself that it would never happen, she and her husband Myron would never be blessed with a boy, her womb only grew girls, babies who sprouted blossoms rather than stalks, and so when she sees a baby boy being aborted she often feels angry and sad and can't keep her mouth closed, several patients have complained about her unsolicited comments, and as Alicia quietly rehashes a catalog of outdated arguments, repeating herself, treading already well-trodden ground, Susan grabs her hand and yanks it, trying to put an end to the murmur that's been licking at her ear this whole time, and Alicia does in fact fall silent, not because of anything Susan did but because she's just bitten her tongue and the pain is sharp and piercing—though now that the nurse has stopped spinning her web of incomprehensible logic, a chant from outside grows louder, encircling the clinic, coming from the synchronized mouths of a crowd of identical people who have gathered on the front steps holding signs dipped in hate, wearing round buttons with Christian slogans on their lapels, shouting their demands that all these Satanic clinics close their doors once and for all, doctors shouldn't be allowed to destroy human lives just like that—it's a frightening sight, boys with buzz cuts and short-sleeved white shirts, black ties, black pants, and dress shoes, and the girls, all blond, in impeccably ironed skirts and pastel jackets, with matching handbags and nondescript flats, and they're all brandishing their own missionary truth, the Book of Mormon and the Pearl of Great Price, waving the books at the handful of surprised passersby who wonder what on earth is happening in their calm, quiet suburb, then hastening away as quickly as possible, trying to keep a safe distance, and before the second-generation Greek American sheriff of Cherry Hill, Nick Pappas, can bring police backup, the clinic door opens a few inches, since the director believes in radical democracy and has the foolish hope of engaging the protestors in dialogue, and when the protesters catch sight of her a dozen eggs, a bucket of red paint, and a smelly vial come hurtling toward the building and splatter with rage over the exterior walls, and the boys and girls step backwards and line up to retreat—and just as surely as they came, the pious ducklings return to their nest, the Church of Jesus Christ of Latter-Day Saints two blocks away, built in honor of the angel Nephi and the great founder and prophet Joseph Smith, who was born in 1805 in the not too distant city of Sharon, Vermont, and grew up in biblical Palmyra, New York.

The Cherry Hill police were glaringly slow in responding, in contrast to their recent record of impressive timeliness and effectiveness on the job, so no arrests were made and no charges pressed, the clinic's director didn't want to prolong what she hoped would be an isolated, unfortunate event of a medieval character, though the local TV station kept the hubbub alive by buttonholing passersby and asking for their views on the event, and the interviewees made the most of these fifteen seconds of fame, handing down long-winded opinions on abortion and anything else that crossed their minds, and when everyone had finally cleared out and the rain had stopped and those trapped inside no longer had to deal, on top of everything else, with the monotonous sound of raindrops hitting the foggy windowpane, an eerie twilight outlined the reflection of the nurse Alicia's round figure in the glass as she walked Susan to the door, where a taxi was waiting that had been called ages ago, and though everything had ended as suddenly as it had begun, for a moment Susan felt like the bloody stain on the door was witness to a heinous, premeditated murder, and the awful stench from the vial of butyric acid made her stomach churn even more, bathing her clothes in a cold sweat, and just as she was getting into the taxi Susan doubled over and fainted, and when she woke up cocooned in her own double bed she discovered that something strange had happened: she had entirely lost her sense of smell, she was sure it was gone for good and accepted it as a divine punishment whose consequences she would carry for the rest of her life, and so she lay back down feeling much calmer than before, because, thank heavens, she and God could call it even.

VI

I have said that the soul is not more than the body,
And I have said that the body is not more than the soul,
And nothing, not God, is greater to one than one's self is,
And whoever walks a furlong without sympathy walks to
   his own funeral drest in his shroud ...
WALT WHITMAN

The ruckus on the Benjamin Franklin Bridge as the fireworks were bursting and snapshots were being taken had as sole target and moral instigator one Antonis Kambanis, commonly known as Nondas. The slim redhead, now the slightly less tender age of twenty, was howling and wailing, shaking her clenched fists threateningly at those standing nearby, and the cooler-headed among them pulled her off to the side and tried in vain, if not to reason with her, at least to calm her down, because an incident like this during the wedding celebrations for two pillars of the community was a bad omen, if you believed in that kind of thing, and Reverend Leone certainly didn't view the developments in a good light, since superstitions of all sorts, apart from being crumbs tossed to appease the masses, were secret Cassandras sounding the alarm, and so he walked ponderously to the edge of the bridge and waited for things to settle down, while Mrs. Mecca, curious and meddlesome by nature, told her girls to stay with their father and cautiously approached the strange creature, who seemed entirely unable to speak—and in fact, as she learned from certain idle but well-informed bystanders, this raging girl was a deafmute, a distant cousin of Bobby O'Ryan's who worked as a maid in one of the imposing homes along Cooper Street, a home that belonged to a well-known architect named Hyland, whose wife Sarah had taken the girl in when she was quite young, because what could be better than a servant who can't talk back or gossip about her employers, and thus Helga had become an irreplaceable fixture in their three-story mansion.

While Mrs. Mecca was trying to figure out what on earth had happened, why this otherwise charming Helga seemed to feel such animosity for their Nondas, her youngest daughter, Anna-Maria, was sending sideways glances at Big Ray's young stooge Neil, with his ruddy cheeks and body chiseled like an ancient Greek sculpture. Neil, meanwhile, was bathed in sweat, his suit was too tight, his collar buttoned too high, his hat too wide and sitting crookedly on his head, he seemed truly out of his depth, a fact that made him even more pleasing to the young ladies, and some of the older ones, too, judging from the glance that came his way from the newly wedded, formerly widowed Monica Sclavi, though that was a fleeting, passing glance, unlike Anna-Maria's playful, lingering gaze, which had taken a long, slow tour of the strapping young man's broad back and powerful shoulders and was now exploring every clothed and unclothed corner of his body, until her father, Tony Mecca, as if by intuition, stepped into her field of vision, blocking her path, interrupting her project of mapping that corporeal terrain, and sent her off to find Pepito and have him fetch a pack of unfiltered Camels. As the sulking girl dragged her feet through the crowd looking for thickheaded Pepito, she suddenly found Neil standing smack dab in front of her, giving her what looked like a knowing wink, maybe he'd seen her looking at him, only who could have snitched, and why was he leering at her like that, what nerve, and then he stepped closer, touched her hand, and whispered in her ear—and just then Mrs. Mecca, weaving her way back to her husband, displeased with what she now knew people had been saying behind her back about Nondas, bumped awkwardly and inelegantly into her daughter, and cried out wearily, "Dammit, didn't I tell you not to move a muscle?"—but Neil had already managed to slip away into the churning crowd, leaving a lingering aura that wrapped itself around the girl slowly and torturously, a portent of trouble to come, he'd whispered something about late-night revels on Petty Island, and Anna-Maria wondered why she and her girlfriends hadn't heard about them before, they knew all the secret spots, and most importantly, how was she going to get there without a boat or escort who would keep the expedition a secret, she couldn't go alone, it was too risky, she'd have to find someone to take her, and as she'd looked him up and down it occurred to her that Nondas Kambanis was the most likely candidate, none of her father's real right-hand men would do it, even asking them would be a dicey proposition, they were sure to rat on her and she'd find herself in hot water before she even went—but the plan was already taking shape in her head and she was convinced that fortune favors the bold, she just had to make sure her meddling mother didn't catch wind, she was always sticking her nose in where it didn't belong.

Mrs. Mecca sneezed three times in a row, her intolerance for dust was legendary. Then she renewed her zealous attack on the furniture with a dust cloth, murmuring an old tune about a hopeless, unrequited love, opened the shutters and cracked the windows to let in a bit of fresh air, this year's humidity had exhausted them, it was the hottest summer she could remember of all her years in Camden, when the discomfort of an intolerably long series of stuffy nights and suffocating days dissolved in a refreshing breeze that suddenly rustled the woven curtains and brushed any remaining dust off the walls and light fixtures, and she felt an unexpected calm that was entirely new to her, as if all her household chores had been taken care of all at once. Meanwhile, her younger daughter Anna-Maria was in the garden talking to Nondas, whom they'd asked to lie low for a few days, fearing retaliation after the hullaballoo on the bridge, though Bobby O'Ryan didn't seem particularly moved by the plight of his distant deafmute cousin, on the contrary he'd called her a hysterical lunatic in front of everyone; her older daughter Costanza, God help her, was reading yet another novel in the attic, this time by some strange British nobody named Woolf; her husband was flipping distractedly through the afternoon *Courier Post* in the funeral home that, due to the oppressive heat of the past few days, had opened early again tonight; and on the northwest pier Pepito and Sergio were loading the moonshine they had bottled two days ago into Big Ray's truck as Big Ray took a quick nap in the passenger seat, since Neil, his buff and chiseled stooge, was sitting behind the wheel and could ward off danger as needed.

Neil had been on edge since the previous morning, when Bobby O'Ryan told him that a crew from New York had been combing the entire state of Pennsylvania looking for him—and when Neil pretended to have no idea what he was talking about, Bobby said those boys were pretty rough and they were letting on that they'd all been in on some robbery on a train from New York to Memphis, only Neil had run off with the loot and hid it in a safe deposit box at the bank, and Neil said that was nuts, they were trying to pin something on him but none of it was true, it was all just a smokescreen, rumors to muddy the waters, the whole mess could be traced back to a certain mulatto woman and one hell of a wager that he was still paying for, and he took off his right shoe and showed him the scar, two toes severed at the joint, "I still remember the cleaver coming down," and Bobby straightened the brim of his hat as he made a sign with his eyes, "Enough," and Neil fell silent and stroked his tommy gun, just as he's doing now, because that gun is his support, his crutch in these tough moments of inner contemplation—it never lets him down when he has to take care of other people's dirty laundry, either, and Big Ray—who is in fact huge, it's not just a name—whirls around in the uncomfortable passenger seat, opens his eyes wide, and barks "You still loading? We've got other jobs to do," through smoke-stained teeth that won't last another five years, soon enough they'll start dropping like rotten blackberries, and with the tip of his tongue he pokes at the tiny fractures and black cavities, testing his endurance for pain, because there's no way in hell he'd ever go to a dentist, the thought of someone bending down over his head, in control, laying siege, is terrible to him, and he gives a swift kick to the door and starts to shout, they've got reefer to pick up, and opium and dope, for Christ's sake they need to get a move on, it's almost dawn and they're still here fucking dawdling, "We're never working with these Italian Casanovas again, not in a million years, a million fucking years!"

Anna-Maria Mecca was devastated that stupid Nondas, that sullen, clumsy, ugly mug of a Nondas, hadn't fallen into her trap, on the contrary he'd said straight-out that he didn't want to get mixed up in anything, had no intention of getting swept up in the tornado he saw on the horizon, the most he could promise was to keep his mouth shut if she would just leave him in peace, and she now wondered if this Greek was going to blackmail her, too, he really did have a criminal face, and dammit, he had her under his thumb, she'd gone and walked right into it like a novice, and there was nowhere else to turn, she thought for a moment about asking Pepito or Sergio, but she knew she'd just get herself into even hotter water, and her girlfriends absolutely refused, it was too scary and dangerous, and besides, there were pirates and robbers on the island, phantoms and spirits that ambushed the unsuspecting, making them shudder and squeal. Anna-Maria wasn't afraid of that kind of imagined fiend, and she certainly wasn't going to turn back at the very first bump in the road, so she rolled herself a cigarette and smoked it down, then stormed up the stairs, heading to her room, and as she passed the door to the attic she heard a faint creaking and an open book slamming emphatically shut, and a silly yet brilliant idea came to her, that she might be able to convince her older sister, of course she'd need to invent a white lie or two, but Costanza was her sister, her own blood, and what could possibly go wrong on a little excursion like this—and so she flew up the attic stairs two at a time before she could change her mind, weaving together the strands of their nighttime intrigue in her mind as she went.

Costanza Mecca didn't rush to respond to her younger sister's request, just pursed her lips until the faint line of a vertical vein appeared on her forehead, she'd been deep in thought when Anna-Maria burst into her bedroom, just when a thousand uncertainties were flooding her heart and she felt her body waking from a deep slumber, her hands burning with the heat of a knowledge she'd never suspected, and now here the evidence was right at her fingertips, carefully hidden in the pages of her book, and the printed words, which she had underlined a first, second, third, even fourth time, witnessed and confirmed her agitation, and for a moment, that very moment, the room seemed flooded with light, and for just an instant, the time it takes for a flame to devour a match, a whole host of unspoken things came to life, and a deeper meaning briefly shone, only to die out again with the first knock on the door, or perhaps it wasn't a knock but her own heart pounding loudly enough to give her away, her palms were sweating, there were things locked tightly within her, things she'd prefer not to know, a part of her wished she could close the book, silence Mrs. Dalloway, erase the words that seemed to have been written specifically for her, while Anna-Maria, bouncing on her sister's bed, begged Costanza to come with her, and to answer her right away, not to keep her waiting a moment longer, and Costanza slowly nodded yes, her delicate lips forming a faint, graceful smile, which unconditionally welcomed and accepted all that would follow from this decision.

That same evening, shortly after ten, with the Meccas' house wrapped in darkness, Costanza and Anna-Maria set out by foot for a cousin's house five blocks away; it was Sonia's birthday and she was having a party for her friends in the garden, which the two sisters intended to use as their cover. Sonia was turning twenty-four and was still unmarried, in fact marriage wasn't even a priority, she wanted to study art history at Vassar and travel to Europe, to see the world and live a grand, adventurous life, and Sonia's mother thought she might die of disgrace, having a daughter on the shelf was the worst of all curses, their walks to church on Sunday and around the neighborhood were always dogged by whispers about poor Sonia, how sad it was that she hadn't had the luck of other girls her age, and Mrs. Sorenti couldn't bear the shame, she felt as if she were carrying around some terrible stigma, some angry pimple that refused to burst—but as the Mecca girls entered the garden, Mrs. Sorenti took some comfort in the sight of Costanza, because when all was said and done, her niece was even worse off, an unapproachable old maid at twenty-five, and Sonia's mother placed her hopes in the merciful Lord her protector, because she knew she was a good Christian, she'd never missed even a single church service, things would surely work out in the end, and she crossed herself and took refuge in the kitchen, she couldn't stand all this youth humming with life, her daughter's friends were giving her a headache with their loud voices and outsized laughter.

Sonia introduced her cousins to the group, and with a wink sat her childhood friend Matteo beside Costanza, who didn't seem the least bit moved by her cousin's initiative. Sonia had an enormous personality that swept everyone and everything up in its wake, and she had developed a rather militant air, rattling on about women's rights, workers' wages, and the power of unions, she talked like a man and never gave in, had strong opinions and was quick to anger, and though men her age looked on her with admiration and perhaps a dose of desire and fear, Sonia had a profound talent that often characterizes vibrant, dynamic women, for wanting only men who would never give her a second glance, who were bothered by something in her irrepressible, unmanageable nature, and so her choices felt unbearably limited and unavoidably predetermined, and she kept getting swept up in romances that came on suddenly like summer storms and ended just as quickly, lasting barely long enough for the rain to quench the thirsty soil. Soon after the sisters arrived at the party Costanza got up and went to the kitchen on the pretext of wanting a glass of water, and for a moment she stood in a daze at the window, looking out over the garden, the dahlias and hollyhocks, and curled her fingers into tight fists as a feeling of utter despair came over her—what an uninspired life she was living!—then she jolted her wrist as if suddenly shaking off an invisible yoke, and as she spun around to head back outside, she tripped over a kitchen stool and fell against the corner of the counter, cutting her eyebrow just a bit, and the hot blood flowed down her pale face, making her look almost pretty.

Costanza began to sob, not because she was in pain, but because she now had an excuse to cry without shame in front of all these people, she had every right and reason, and her younger sister was kneeling before her, speaking to her sweetly to ease her pain, and Sonia held her hand and told her not to worry, it was just a scratch, really, it wouldn't leave a scar, and the young men in the group had come close enough to offer their support without getting wrapped up in the personal drama taking place before them. Mrs. Sorenti ran to bring help, and since Dr. Zakolski was too far away to get to quickly, she went two houses down and knocked on the door of Mrs. Hocevar, who at thirty years old was already both a widow and a successful head nurse at West Jersey Hospital, which stood silent and imposing at the corner of Mt. Efraim and Atlantic Avenues.

Mrs. Hocevar had recently been suffering from insomnia. Shortly after her husband was killed in the Twelfth Battle of the Isonzo in the fall of 1917, she took whatever they had in cash and jewelry and boarded a boat for the Land of Promise without a word to anyone, and though it had been almost eleven years since her Croatian husband had been drafted into the Austro-Hungarian army of his imperial majesty Kaiser Wilhelm II, she had never wanted to remarry. After all, her experience of marriage had been fairly unpleasant, bordering on nonexistent, and while she didn't shout it from the rooftops, she knew she had been given a second chance to shape her life as she wanted it to be, because there's no greater thing than freedom, and in America, despite the puritanism and jingoism she had encountered, she was a woman with no roots or ties, respected by all, thanks in large part to the humanitarian nature of her work, and the only thing that hinted at her exotic Balkan background was her weighty surname, whose choppy consonants sounded like someone sawing away at an oak tree— but that night, as she twisted and turned in bed, plagued with a resurgence of guilt for having left parents and children and a brother behind to emigrate without even saying goodbye, there was a knock at the door, and to her great joy and relief she grabbed her medical bag and followed Mrs. Sorenti through the night, because there was no better sleeping potion than an exhausted body, and when she walked through the house and out to the back garden her gaze fell on Costanza Mecca, on the young woman's deep sadness and eyes that threw sparks, on her somber face made prettier by the cut crowning her left eyebrow, and Mrs. Hocevar's breath caught, she felt a pang in her heart and slowed her step, it was as if she were seeing herself ten years younger hunched on the stone steps of her family home in Gradiška, Slovenia, waiting for something dramatic to happen, something that would push her to the edge of a cliff, something that would help her finally decide to dare the impossible—and just then, like the déjà vu of a battle that was never fought, their eyes met, sealing their first moment of mutual recognition.

The wound was in fact quite minor, and Mrs. Hocevar's experienced hands cleaned and dressed it and prescribed a day of rest, suggesting that Costanza come by the hospital if she had a chance, "tomorrow, if possible," otherwise she herself could stop by on her way home, and Anna-Maria asked anxiously, "Is it serious?" and Mrs. Hocevar shook her head, "No, but you can't be too careful," and Costanza Mecca sensed something playful, almost incongruously alluring in Mrs. Hocevar's warm voice and gestures, and she had a sudden intuition that reality held a second level in store for the select few, a level that had just revealed itself to her in all its thrilling extent—and as she examined Mrs.

Hocevar's strong hands, straight posture, and the dimples in her cheeks, Costanza felt as if she had known this woman a long time, and Mrs. Sorenti gladly jotted down the address of the Mecca home, then took Mrs. Hocevar aside to give her a little something for her trouble, but the nurse politely declined the offer, "Goodness, no," she said, and just as she was about to leave the house, she turned and tried to catch Costanza's eye, but the girl was hunched over staring at her pale palms, smiling indifferently at Matteo's compliments, that the cut on her eyebrow and the orange streak of ammonia made her no less beautiful, and in fact even more desirable than before.

As so often happens in life, Anna-Maria Mecca was unable to follow through on the plans she'd made that afternoon, and perhaps she let them go on purpose, for the night was warm and the company enjoyable, the wine and conversation flowed pleasantly, and her interest was held by the teasing banter of a young man named Nino seated to her left, he was almost handsome, with rugged features, he reminded her of an actor in the silent cinema, at least when he wasn't opening his mouth to fill the awkward silences, and he made a good salary as a real-estate agent, he'd already bought his own car and had dreams, he wanted to drive across country and settle in Hollywood, he was sure he'd do well there, the climate on the West Coast suited him, and as she leaned closer to him over the canapés and mushroom caps stuffed with cheese, Anna-Maria pictured herself in the passenger seat, and her face lit up as she imagined their life together in the City of Angels. Meanwhile, as she sat there laughing and talking with Nino, Neil was holed up in Pastor Moore's apartment, riddled with anxiety, his mafia friends had been tipped off that he was in Camden, and Big Ray, who had no desire to get mixed up in any tricky business with the sidekicks of the powerful Don Vito, a rising star in the mob world, had told Neil to get packed for a little vacation because just before dawn a white van would come to take him as far as the lakes bordering Canada, and from there he'd keep going on his own as far as Ottawa, and when he crossed over into the land of maple and marmots he should forget all about Big Ray, Neil was on his own from now on, and if he knew what was good for him he'd take the first boat back to Europe, disappear off the face of the earth for at least a decade, until the dust settled and the debt was forgotten, and Neil, who harbored no ill will toward Big Ray, did not object, and did in fact leave, at least for a bit—only to return to New York three months later, grumpy and broke, and one night after racking up a respectable tab at the 21 Club, he stood up, raised his .45, and took ten bullets in a row before falling from his own, the last.

VII

the sack of kittens
sinking in the icy creek
increases the cold
NICK VIRGILIO

Basil Kambanis met the realtor at the diner to discuss the next steps for putting it up for sale, with
the house soon to follow, and Nino Cavani Junior,
second son of Nino Cavani and Anna-Maria Mecca,
gave the place a once-over to set an initial asking
price, weighing its age and atmosphere, calculating
property values in the neighborhood and the imme-
diacy of his new client's needs, he knew Basil didn't
want to see the efforts of a lifetime paved over into
a parking lot, at least not if he could avoid it, and
Nino Cavani told him he'd do his best, but Basil
shouldn't pin his hopes on a better offer, and should
definitely consider the one in hand. As for the
house, Nino was pretty sure he'd be able to get a
good price for it over the next few months, he just
needed to know they were moving forward, there

was no time like the present, after all, but Basil didn't budge, "First the diner and then the house, we've been over that"—and Nino held out a hand and their lukewarm handshake sealed a certain tenuous agreement and put the cherry on the cake of a rash, self-destructive, vengeful impulse, whose drive to devour didn't bode well.

Nino Cavani smooths down his shirt, which looks expensive but was actually purchased at the outlet mall in the northern suburbs of Philadelphia, and retreats with his head bowed, the money isn't as good as it used to be, business is on the decline, he's having to take on sales that will earn him almost no profit, second-rate places that require two or three times the effort for almost no return, just enough to cover his gas—stinking Arabs, how high can the price of a gallon go?—and he's got his mom on his case, too, eighty years old with one foot in the grave after a couple of strokes and still nagging him about not being married or having a family, how can he manage a house on his own, what does he eat, who keeps things clean, all in the hope he'll take her in as his permanent roommate, he's at the end of his rope, she calls every day and lets the phone ring until he picks up, she's got the receptionist at the Capri nursing home wrapped around her finger, sitting like a statue by the phone to place all those calls, he suspects the spending money he gives his mom each month goes straight into the woman's pocket, they've teamed up to make his life a living hell, and it's even worse now that his older brother got married and their mother has only one bachelor son to focus her energies on, though his brother might actually have it worse since his in-laws live right next door, meaning he's got twice the headache, a marriage and in-laws, too, but though she's definitely declining, their mother is still as clever as a fox and knows how to sweet-talk people into doing what she wants—"For Pete's sake, fuck it all," he says, and gets into the car and steps on the gas, and Basil looks out the window of the diner and sees burnt rubber staining the pavement, dust rising and hanging for a moment in the air. He's made up his mind, all that's left is to share the news, today or tomorrow, next week, next month or the one after, he's going to let the diner go to the dogs, and then the house, and it's just a matter of time before he puts the divorce in motion—he's decided, made up his mind, he and Susan have nothing in common anymore, and if there was one thing that might hypothetically have tied them together even now, well, she just got rid of that, too.

Minnie and Leto are playing Pacman at Bill's Arcade, known around town for its huge collection of coin-operated sports games and pinball machines that sneak into your pocket and eat up your allowance when you're looking the other way. Today is Minnie's birthday, she's turning twelve, and since Leto has always been good at wrangling things out of her parents, as soon as she smelled an opportunity she started badgering Minnie to ask for an all-expenses-paid afternoon at Bill's, and Minnie gave in because otherwise Leto would never have left her in peace, and now she's standing and watching Leto push yet another coin through the slot of the gluttonous yellow machine, while in the depths of the narrow arcade Susan is drinking a lemonade with extra sugar stirred in, chasing the tiny crystals around with her straw in annoyance, because in all these years it never occurred to her how inseparable the link is between taste and smell, and for the past few weeks she's been eating everything in sight, seeking even the tiniest trace of flavor in the sweetest and saltiest foods, but the only thing that slides down her gullet is a vague synthetic sense that fills her mouth and swells her stomach with biodegradable plastic.

It's Minnie's turn to play Pacman, and just as she did five minutes ago, she again hands over her coin and cedes her turn to the impatient Leto, who's set herself the goal of eating all the cherries and strawberries and apples and melons and getting to the very end of the game, conquering all the levels and the annoying multicolored ghosts that chase her up and down and take away her lives one by one, and Minnie seizes the opportunity to slip away from Susan's notice and Leto's ravenous desires and goes out to the street on her own, steps carefully over the narrow, cracked sidewalk, then quickly crosses the street and ducks into a tiny fast-food joint she's had her eye on for a while, with a banner over the door reading *Por Suerte* and a framed flag of Puerto Rico that's slightly crumpled at the edges on one wall, all she's been able to think about since she set foot in Gateway is sneaking over to this hole-in-the-wall place where her brother sometimes hangs out and ordering a side of fried plantains in the hope she might buck up, grow a shade taller, and regain all the things and time she's lost, even if just for a moment, and Diego, a knucklehead with a spotty mustache and backwards Phillies cap who's standing behind the counter, passes her a serving of freshly fried plantains and a bit of rice and beans and chicken that's left over from yesterday and will be thrown out otherwise, and starts asking where she lives, if she's new to the neighborhood, if she's been following the feats of the Phillies in the World Series, how the legendary third baseman Mike Schmidt led them to their very first championship, crushing Kansas City—"Four games to two, can you believe it?"—as Minnie chews one piece of fried plantain after another, and each bite is a distant regret that sticks in her throat, for something she said or something she didn't do, for all the bad, ugly thoughts she ever wished would come true, and now she wants to take them all back, but as much as she might like to believe in the miracle of the fried plantain, she knows very well that her father left them, has another family, maybe even a happy one, in that shining city over the bridge, and her mother won't ever come back down from heaven, she's surely found a nice, comfortable place up there in the sky to live out her old age, and if her brother were ever to show up he would just bring trouble, curses, and threats, even if she forgave everything he did with her whole heart, the braid he chopped off, the air gun pellets, the sly punches and secret wounds, the stolen allowance, and the vow of silence he made her take, flexing the butterfly tattoo on his right arm, threatening to kill her in her sleep if she ever told their mother that he snuck out at night, or where he went while the two of them were sleeping in the ground-floor apartment in Centerville, which is now utterly empty of voices and life and furniture, too, dark and unrented, because as soon as they saw the lacquer coffin coming out through the door, the neighbors went in and grabbed all the appliances, and then the sofa and coffee table and chairs, and finally the cheap dishes that had been left behind like animal skeletons, fake porcelain corpses in the cupboards.

But things have changed so much, and Minnie is no longer afraid of Pete and his stupid gang, their swagger and code of silence, and as Diego scrapes some sticky crumbs off the counter, Minnie throws him the bait, "What time do the Quiñones meet at the playground?" and without batting an eye Diego leans over slyly and looks straight at her, "Who's asking?" and Minnie answers, "Pete's sister wants to see him," and Diego looks her up and down, and Minnie, who has often read the crib sheets her brother used to hide under his beat-up mattress, because the idiot just couldn't learn things by heart, gets up on her knees on the stool and with the most natural, undaunted air asks for the bill, and leaves a whole shiny nickel as tip, which, though it's not her intention, is heavy with innuendos, and now Diego, standing in the weak afternoon sun, is holding the coin in his palm and looking first at it and then at the framed photograph on the wall of a threadbare group of friends posing blurrily for the camera one July at the Centerville public pool, shortly before it closed for good after the strange, unexplained drowning death of one of the five smiling youths in the picture. The rest of them kept their childhood nicknames—Fatso, Don Juan, Junior, and the Mayor—even in their new lives as big-shot crack and dope barons, leaders of the Organization, which was, in fact, impeccably organized, with two off-shoots, the Quiñones and Bookbag, for pushing weed and rock, crack and snow in the schools and projects all over New Jersey, as far as Atlantic City and even New York.

When Minnie returns to Bill's Arcade it's as if she never left, Susan has nodded off at her little table with a pile of newspapers from the day before yesterday blaring the news of John Lennon's murder across the front page, and Leto is still at it, emitting little shouts and cries of joy over the record she just broke and the new level she just got to on the concave screen, and Minnie, who thinks video games are boring, circles the arcade twice and then goes over to Susan, tugs gently on her sleeve and asks, in all seriousness, "What's the difference between eleven and twelve?" and Susan wakes with a gasp from a deep sleep and says, "One more candle on the cake," then pauses, gaining momentum, and adds, "and I bet those two missing teeth will come in," and Minnie sticks her tongue through the gaps in her gums as Susan grabs her gently by the wrist, "and maybe you'll become a woman, too, this year or next," and Minnie lets out a shriek and cups her hand over her open mouth, because Susan has said something you're not supposed to say, or at least she doesn't want to hear, "You mean the Reds will appear?" she asks, terrified that her terrible suspicion might be confirmed, that "Sooner or later the Reds will raise the Russian flag," and as she overheard the son of a recently cuckolded and newly divorced Republican candidate for city council saying at school a few years back, "All women are by nature betrayers, potential anarcho-autonomists, and secret communists, from the moment they raise the red flag," and as Leto plays her very last coin with complete concentration and masterful sleight of hand, managing to run the virtual gauntlet all the way to the fifty-first level, the lights suddenly flicker and the power goes out for all of three seconds, and when it comes back on the dreaded white letters are flashing on her screen, *GAME OVER*, and then, *INSERT COIN*.

It's Sunday evening a bit past seven and a thick December darkness has fallen over the street and the signs on the accountants' and lawyers' offices, the hazy lights of the white marquee reading *Ariadne* are reflected in the glass as the bus on the Dudley line that ends in Cooper-Grant skates past on the deserted avenue, and Basil Kambanis is jotting down the week's shifts and trying to figure out what on earth they'll do tomorrow with Sally out sick, something in her throat and lungs, the doctors said they'll have to run some tests, and Veronica who suffers from migraines and panic attacks can't possibly manage on her own, or maybe she can, they'll have to sit down and figure it out together—"Veronica?"—but what the heck, he's selling the place anyhow, so who cares, they can bulldoze it, pave it over, it's Sunday evening and there's not a soul in the diner or on the streets, last week around this time there was a break-in at the dime store across the way and no one even noticed, the police came and filled out a few forms, collected a few signatures, and then left as quickly as they'd come, tail between their legs, it's not even eight and he doesn't usually close up shop until nine but he might as well leave an hour early, there's no use hanging around—"Veronica?"—and as he's looking around for her, the door to the diner opens and a gust of wind fans the grills, makes the ceiling fans spin and the lamps sway, they're expecting a snowstorm tonight and the temperature is going to drop down to twenty, he's lived his whole life on the east coast and has never gotten used to the cold, eight months of winter, two of summer, and the other two months are wildcards toying with his nerves, flipping from cold to hot and back again, and the snow never melts, just freezes and turns into a crystalline mud, a gigantic amoeba spreading over the city and voraciously devouring streets and sidewalks, houses and cars.

That night the snow never stopped, in just a few hours nearly two feet had fallen, and there wasn't a person around who didn't stand for a moment by a door or window to watch in wonder before looking back down to pull on their boots and gloves, who didn't let their mind wander, thinking about the deafening silence of snow, how a snowflake falls and disappears, and Basil Kambanis stands and speaks quietly in the hall leading to the living room, right beside the tiny guest bathroom the size of a closet, and Susan is leaning against the wall listening to him with her hands folded across her chest, she doesn't have the energy to get involved in his petty accounting and doesn't really want to, either, and every measured comment he makes is a tiny hook of silence that Susan swallows down, he says he doesn't want anything, she can keep the money from the house and the diner on the condition that she won't ask for alimony, the divorce will be mutual, "And the girls?" Susan interrupts, and Basil lowers his head and kicks at an invisible snowflake stuck to the toe of his boot, which he forgot to take off, so he's now tracked melting snow all down the hall and through the living room, "You know best," he answers, and yes, in fact, she knows that each snowflake is entirely unique in its composition, and that the snow will linger in the city until March, maybe even April, and at some point the river will freeze in places, just like on Christmas night in 1776 when George Washington crossed the Delaware with twenty-four hundred men and won the first important battle for the Continental Army, the Battle of Trenton, and all these are minor events that took place and were written down, just like the fact that her husband is a coward who decided to turn tail and flee as soon as the going got tough, and she doesn't even care, because something inside her has frozen, she can feel the stiffness from her toes to the nape of her neck, and both of them hear the creaking of the bathroom door, which opens just a crack at first and then is flung wide open as Leto emerges from the darkness with a huge stack of Panini sports cards that she's planning on trading the next day at school, little cards that will send them back in time three whole years to the 1978 World Cup in Argentina, John Travolta in *Grease*, and, by all accounts, the happiest, most carefree summer in the history of the entire planet.

Leto stands between them like a bridge floating over the murky waters of a turbulent river, she simply refuses to break down and start crying, she won't do them the favor, and she won't have an asthma attack either, she just clenches her cards tighter, crushing the smiling face of Daniel Passarella, then takes off at a run, shoots down the hall to the living room where she flops onto her temporary, uncomfortable bed that's out in the open, exposed to the elements, to the whims of their family weather, still in her shoes and all her clothes like a shipwrecked sailor, and she wraps herself up in the blanket all the way up to her head, trying not to leave even the slightest gap where washed-up seaweed could slip in and wrap her in its slimy, disgusting tentacles, and when Basil kneels beside her and whispers a few words of entirely unhelpful grown-up wisdom, Leto pretends to be sleeping, squeezing her eyes shut so tightly that her mouth crinkles at the edges and her face fills with premature wrinkles, creating a precocious image of an old little girl that's so funny and out of place that it couldn't possibly evoke any feeling other than deep sadness.

Minnie doesn't plan on sleeping tonight, she wants to stay up and finish her homework for tomorrow's classes, she's fallen behind, especially in geometry, and now she's using her pencil to calculate the surface area of a handful of chocolate cookies that look in the illustration like flying saucers emerging from a futuristic chocolate-cookie machine, their diameter is .6 of an inch, and her mind runs in circles around the crunchy almondy rays, eventually calculating approximately 8 square inches of imaginary surface that leaves a full, sweet flavor in her mouth, and she's ready to move on to the circumference of a car tire and the surface area of a cross-shaped figure trapped inside a cute but also kind of complex square, but before she tackles that difficult task, as she chews the bland head of her number 2 pencil, Leto pushes open the door with the blanket shielding her red, puffy eyes, draped over her whole body like an ancient cloak hiding bad news in its folds, and collapses onto the bed facedown beside Minnie and falls asleep almost instantly, because here in her room with Minnie she feels safe, and Minnie, whose eyes are heavy with the exhaustion of so many late nights, lets the note-book drop to the floor and turns off the light, and the two girls sleep side by side, their breath slowly synchronizing in the darkness of night.

VIII

How they are provided for upon the earth, (appearing
  at intervals;)
How dear and dreadful they are to the earth;
How they inure to themselves as much as to any—
What a paradox appears their age;
How people respond to them, yet know them not;
How there is something relentless in their fate, all times;
How all times mischoose the objects of their adulation
  and reward,
And how the same inexorable price must still be paid
  for the same great purchase.

WALT WHITMAN

It didn't take long for the friendship between young
Costanza Mecca and Mrs. Hocevar to make waves in
the small city, perhaps because people are always
jealous of happiness, and everyone wanted to know
why Miss Mecca's face was no longer pale but blush-
ing and full of life, and as the younger Mecca sister
was increasingly plagued by a dead-end romance
and an impending marriage that would be the end

result of major obstinacy and minor interests, the older sister had a new openness in her gaze and glowed with touching simplicity—though soon enough, perhaps inevitably, her small, harmless secret was discovered, thanks to a combination of carelessness and bad faith, when Nondas Kambanis, at the request of the Meccas' soon-to-be son-in-law Nino Cavani, and of course enticed by the generous wad of cash that came with it, began to trail his boss's daughter and saw Costanza Mecca going into Mrs. Hocevar's house on several occasions, though if he hadn't been made suspicious by the wagging tongues, he wouldn't have found anything particularly shifty or strange about two grown women spending time together, chatting beside a small unlit fireplace, or on a tiny back porch surrounded by potted vegetables, knitting scarves or the sleeves of future sweaters at the end of summer in the company of an ancient, peevish, nine-lived alley cat. Evening after evening he waited patiently on the sidewalk hidden by the thick trunk of a tree, and just when he'd lost all hope of ever having something interesting to report, what he'd been waiting for finally happened: one evening as Mrs. Hocevar was bidding Miss Mecca goodnight, she embraced her warmly, as always, and then as they lingered in the half-open door of the two-story house their hands tangled tightly together, and Mrs. Hocevar's other hand reached out to stroke Costanza's cheek, and she kissed her gently, carefully, on the mouth, as if the younger woman might break, and Costanza blushed, feeling dizzy, but didn't pull away, just felt for the door with her hand and gently closed it, and didn't come back outside until the mellifluous bells of Our Lady of Mt. Carmel had struck twelve.

Nondas Kambanis wasn't a rat—he may have been an ignorant coward, and a bit naive about the facts of life, but he certainly wasn't cut from squealer's cloth. What he'd seen had shocked and disturbed him, and he would gladly have discussed it in private with the Mecca pater familias, but the issue was a delicate one, of a particular nature, and his instinct told him not to get mixed up in other people's affairs, especially when it came to love, that it would only get him in hot water and bring recriminations raining down on his head, and so he sealed his mouth tightly and kept the secret to himself, until he finally opened Aeolus's sack one night when he was down with the crew in the basement bottling grappa, and after hours of breathing in fumes that could bring even corpses to their feet, and of course the occasional sip for quality control, his head was spinning like a top, and in the flow of conversation the scalawag let on a bit more than he should have, saying how he couldn't imagine what any two women did in bed together, much less Mrs. Hocevar and Miss Mecca—and Nino Cavani, who knew perfectly well what two women could get up to in bed, and was still fairly sober and level-headed, didn't lose an instant, but seized the opportunity to set his terms for the marriage contract, including the inviolable condition that if Costanza weren't cured of her unnatural inclinations, Anna-Maria's engagement would be called off and the wedding would never take place, Nino simply couldn't overlook something like that in the family, since who could be sure any future children born of the union might not carry the same shame and stigma in their blood.

The wailing and lamentation lasted three days at the Mecca home after Costanza Mecca bent and broke, admitted her guilt and her vile nature, weathered her mother's shouts and threats and her father's sullen scowl at having been put in such a difficult position. Mrs. Mecca then decided to take matters into her own hands and, accompanied by Reverend Leone, paid a visit to Mrs. Hocevar and asked, or rather demanded, that she cut off all contact with their innocent little girl—who, meanwhile, was a solid twenty-six, going on twenty-seven —and threatening her neighbor with terrible consequences if she didn't comply, the matter was in danger of assuming grave dimensions, Costanza Mecca's honor was at stake, no prospective husband would want to marry a girl with such a checkered, diseased past, and Reverend Leone, who was at heart a pure and mild-mannered man who hated to see any of his flock wandering from the straight and narrow, invited Mrs. Hocevar to come to confession, repent, and leave behind the life of the sinful harlot, upon which Mrs. Hocevar, who felt she had tolerated quite enough of their insults in her own home, suddenly informed them she'd had enough of their impudence, that what happened in her bed was none of their concern, and she swung the door open rather rudely to show them out —"Goodbye and good riddance"—and Mrs. Mecca gathered her pride, fixed the clips in her wavy hair, took the shocked priest by the arm and, head held high, marched across the few yards of sidewalk back home, taking care not to step in any sneaky mud-puddles.

Though Mrs. Hocevar and Miss Mecca lived in the same city, they never met again. Sometimes that's how fortune will have it, especially in the face of adverse conditions and inauspicious years, fortune requires daring, boldness, sacrifices, and action to keep its wheels spinning, and while Mrs. Hocevar thought of Miss Mecca often, kept her close in her heart and wondered where she might be, what she might be doing, whether she was happy, she never dared to ask outright. After all, the neighborhood had turned against her, people said all kinds of things behind her back, there were rumors of orgies, opium-laced cigarettes, hallucinogenic drinks, moral misconduct of all kinds—though Mrs. Hocevar didn't much mind, she had thrown herself into her job, and on her afternoons off she would visit the public library, even in the depths of winter, and she always found comfort in the paper world of joys and sorrows she found there, while Miss Mecca, now Mrs. Costanza Totti, withered in a hastily arranged marriage that might more appropriately have been called a life sentence, for she held out no hope and had no self-delusions, she knew she had been trapped in the pages of a badly written book, a farce whose storyline was in fact fated soon to run out: just over a year later, Mrs. Totti complained of a steadily worsening indisposition, which her family and friends attributed to her delicate constitution and weak nerves, but in the space of three months, two weeks, and five days, she was confined to bed with terrible pains throughout her whole body, was diagnosed with metastatic breast cancer in mid-August, 1928, and after a gasping, inglorious struggle, on the first Monday in October she closed her eyes for good, secure in the knowledge that she had at least lived a great, novel-worthy love, and was buried, in accordance with her final request, in Harleigh Cemetery, in the same soil and surrounded by the same foliage as her favorite poet and humanist, Walt Whitman, and it was late one night, after midnight, when Mrs. Hocevar, flipping through the previous week's *Courier Post*, came across an obituary for the 28-year-old Costanza Totti, née Mecca, beloved wife, sister, daughter, aunt—and lover, she wanted to add, but her bitter tears kept her from speaking.

Although Nondas Kambanis had merely been a cog in the gears, the last car in the train that led to the scandalous revelation, and certainly hadn't intended to cause all that trouble, he was still taken for a liar and held responsible for the double disaster that had befallen them: since the Mecca family had no one else to blame, and with this second, accursed stigma of cancer running through their blood, their animosity toward Mrs. Hocevar evaporated, or rather was displaced onto another conniving interloper, a foreigner they all now claimed to have disliked from the start, he was always sticking his crooked nose into everything and spreading his vinegar and gall, and from the moment he'd landed on their doorstep out of the blue one evening years earlier they had all been suffering one trial after another. During an urgent family meeting Mrs. Mecca called at Anna-Maria's insistence, they came to the unanimous decision, supported most vocally by Nino Cavani who assumed the role of prosecutor, that they needed to rid themselves of this sycophantic and shameless Greek at the first possible opportunity, to shake off his services—he could go in peace back to wherever he came from, they bore him no ill will, he'd find his way, as so many others had done, and when they'd all agreed and made a common plan in no time at all, they popped open a bottle of red wine they'd been saving in the cellar for just such a celebratory occasion and washed away all their doubts, raised a glass to the rare gifts and innate goodness of the prematurely departed Costanza, and wished with all their hearts that future generations of Meccas would know nothing but joy and prosperity.

The news found Nondas Kambanis in his two-room apartment on Bergen Square, to which Tony Mecca came in person to share the unpleasant tidings, accompanied of course by his irreplaceable henchmen, Sergio and Pepito. A cycle of his life had ended, an era had drawn to a close, November was yet again showing its teeth, and Nondas Kambanis, who would soon become Antonis once more, felt the earth disappearing from beneath his feet, upset not so much about losing a respectable wage and the satisfying craft of making moonshine as he was at losing the goodwill and support of people he'd come to consider his family, who had not only cut him out of their circle but were openly accusing him of deceit, of having dragged an innocent, defenseless girl through the mud of the city's slander, and were even foisting their daughter's illness on him, claiming that his baseless lies had sent her to an early grave. Antonis Kambanis listened, incredulous, to the long list of accusations, then simply asked their forgiveness, silently accepting all the allegations, thanked his boss for the wonderful years he had spent in his employ, and closed the door to sit down and start his life all over from the beginning. He couldn't believe his rotten luck, he must have been doing something wrong, and after spending a sleepless night cycling through the awful, unfair events in his mind, he decided that from then on he would have dealings only with Greeks, because as unscrupulous, crooked, and backwards as they might be, at least they were the devil he knew.

With the savings he'd set aside during his time with the Mecca family, Antonis Kambanis got a small house in East Camden on the border of Cramer Hill and Dudley, where a hundred or so Greeks had cobbled together a little community, with plans in the works for an Orthodox church and a cultural center to house their gatherings and host their events, and with the rest of the money, a fairly respectable sum, he calculated his overhead and potential earnings and decided he was in a position to start a little venture of his own, he'd get a pushcart permit from the city, and since in his opinion either loukoumades or a sausage cart both required a woman's touch, he decided to turn his own scant capital into fruit: apples and oranges in winter, strawberries and cherries in spring, and toward the end of summer, why not, prickly pears, raspberries, blackberries. And that's just what he did, and in under a month he was out on the streets hawking his first goods, and though it was exhausting work and the long hours on his feet took a hefty toll on his calves and back, the money wasn't bad, he could cover his costs and even put a little aside, and since he didn't trust the banks, he just rolled up the bills and shoved them inside his mattress like an old lady would, it was a lesson he'd learned from his mother who had witnessed the bankruptcy of the Greek state in 1893, money is like a sweetheart, you need to keep it close at hand, because it's easy to forget a pair of eyes you never see, and though the siren song of the vast profits being made in 1928 were calling him, Antonis Kambanis never borrowed a cent, never gambled, never invested his earnings in the golden giddiness of the stock market—and so, against all odds, on Black Thursday and Black Tuesday of October, 1929, he came out ahead for the sole reason that he didn't lose out, having kept his cash stashed safe and sound among the feathers of his second-rate mattress.

And while banks and shares collapsed like a huge house of cards, pulling depositors and investors into financial ruin, Antonis Kambanis allowed himself some small enjoyment of the fruits of his labor, which he had saved like the apple of his eye, though he saw that things were going from bad to worse, sales from his cart had fallen sixty or seventy percent in the space of a year, his produce was rotting and he was having to sell it at a third of its retail price, so his profits were slight, a nickel or dime here or there that clinked pleadingly in his ears, and in the summer of 1930 the International Apple Growers Association had the bright idea of distributing their surplus on credit to the unemployed, putting some three hundred homeless salesmen out on the streets with improvised crates to hawk their produce from neighborhood to neighborhood, literally drowning the place in five-cent apples, and Antonis Kambanis cursed his bad fortune and finally threw up his hands, gave his leftover goods to the bands of street urchins who seemed to be everywhere, combing the streets and picking through trash in search of food, and decided to switch gears, left behind the fruit business, and leased a six-by-six hole-in-the-wall in Dudley, where he and a partner from Salonica set up a shoe-repair shop they called Second Chance, and when business got going enough that they were earning a few dimes a day, they hired a down-and-out Levantine seamstress to do some hasty mending and upped their daily income to a half dollar or so, though business was still slow, in first gear on an incline, and just when they had finally managed to step on the gas and start moving, the tank ran out entirely: in 1933 you could wait a week or more to catch sight of a dime, everyone was buying on credit, and the economy slowed to a crawl as Hooverville shanty towns and philanthropic organizations with dozens of volunteers sprang up all over the place, the soup kitchen lines looked like skinny black snakes circling the city, and at the butcher's shop customers begged for an extra morsel of meat under the table, or sent their kids to ask for bones for non-existent dogs—and amid all this misery and gloom, Antonis Kambanis went and fell crashingly, hopelessly, stupidly in love.

IX

family dinner
the lights
too dim
DANIELLE MURDOCH

To Basil and Susan's general amazement, Leto and Minnie have become inseparable, and while at first Susan was doubtful of the sincerity of their friendship, wondering whether and to what degree her daughter might be taking advantage of their young guest's presence, she finally concluded that the two girls were in fact now close, bound by the ties of a strange yet practical friendship, and while at first Leto seemed to have the upper hand, the tables have now turned, so that Minnie is the one who gives the orders and calls the shots, and Basil, who has lost all faith in the safety and shelter of the conjugal hearth and sees everything through a veil of suspicion, is convinced that this about-face is part of some devious plan of Susan's, that the girls are in on it, that they're all trying to outsmart him, wear him down, make him change his mind and stay, but it's not going to work, in fact the more he thinks about it the more stubborn he gets, remembering his first love for a devious, double-crossing girl from Smyrna, his second love for the shy, retiring daughter of a shop owner named Stein, a love he really believed was true and took him nearly two years to get over, and his third, poisonous love for a druggist's daughter that went off the rails shortly before the wedding—and how looking to heal his wounds, he fell face-forward into the clutches of his current wife, Susan, who seems to him tonight like a bird of prey, her fingers curled into talons and lips narrowed into a thin line incapable of letting loose even a crumb of kindness, and his father's old words of advice come back to him amplified, buzzing with feedback in his ear, that second chances are always hollow, made for those who will inevitably want third and fourth chances, too, who won't ever get their fill of failure, "Are you listening, Vassilis, or are you out gathering wool again?"

Vassilis—or Basil, in his own American version—was in fact out gathering wool, he was a sensitive kid who fell in love like a ton of bricks. As a little boy he wanted to be Christ when he grew up, and the other kids made fun of him, tossing curses and rocks, until the age of twelve when his fantasies of being a holy martyr ceased and he started to fill out a bit, metaphorically and literally, growing to five foot ten and stopping for good just around there— and he was handsome, or almost handsome, he was a sweet-talker with mesmerizing honey-colored eyes fringed by long, black, melancholy lashes, he had taken after his mother Rallou from the village of Asomatos on Lesvos, known all over Dudley for her superb physique, her delectable home cooking, and the ouzo she downed by the carafe when she had troubles on her mind, and every so often she would rush out onto the sidewalk, an unrecognizably muddled mess, to heckle passersby with coarse gestures and profanities, and young Basil was constantly worried that his mother might slip and fall again into a drunken state while his father was off at work or running errands, and so he would turn again to his invented prayers, becoming a little Christ again who could withstand pain and offer forgiveness and absolution for the shame and suffering that hounded him.

But the suffering kept coming, and on a quiet summer afternoon at the beginning of June, 1944, as the days were heating up and the bustle in the streets was cooling down, while Antonis Kambanis was at the shop about to tuck into his lunch half an hour later than usual, Rallou wandered out into the street like a ghost, and though she hadn't yet polished off her third half-liter carafe of red wine, she felt a strange dizziness, her legs seemed to go numb, and she fell as if by design in front of the first car to come zooming down the street, and Basil, who had come outside to fetch her back, froze in his tracks, didn't run to help, just stood there staring at his mother's motionless body lying in the street and the driver screaming—and then, certain that his mother was dead, he opened the front door of the house, went inside, closed the door behind him, emptied the carafe into the sink, washed and dried it well, and placed it back in the cupboard, then sat down on the sofa and waited, and when his father came back close to midnight, he shouted at Basil and slapped him hard across the face, a slap to remember: his mother was alive, but paralyzed, and from now on their troubles would know no end.

Basil and his father had neither a strong bond nor any common interests to bring them closer together, Antonis Kambanis had tried several times to teach him the tricks of the trade at the shoe-repair shop, but the boy had no interest in manual work, his natural talent and inclination was for literature, for reading and writing, and though Antonis turned a blind eye, he remained inwardly skeptical, they'd never had any artsy types in the family, but his son was so stubborn and insistent that he at least pretended to give in, and besides, business was flying high, they had built up a small local chain with three Second Chance locations, two of which now belonged to him outright, the economy and industry were booming, America and its allies had won the war, and since Antonis refused to hire an assistant and was always scuttling from store to store to oversee deliveries and manage the accounts, Basil looked after Rallou with a book or notebook in hand, and when he got tired of his lessons, which was happening more and more often, he would pull out his Superman comics, which he practically knew by heart—he may still have had a thing for Christ, but Superman was also here to stay, and he was way cooler and more handsome and actually lived among people, a humble reporter who was also a secret superhero and used his powers for the common good, and at the age of nine, as his paralyzed mother begged him for a glass of strong wine, Basil Kambanis set his sights on becoming a successful reporter whose writing would save the world from its dangerous delusions.

His plans went up in a puff of smoke a year later when he tried his hand at the school newspaper at East Camden Middle School: his full-page articles about poisonous spiders in the Amazon or the lives of the martyred saints were of no interest to anyone, and his long-winded, ruminating style provoked cascading yawns in his readers, who could be counted on the fingers of one hand and were always quite happy to turn the page to a new piece, interested as they were in more tangible, easily digested topics, what ice-cream shop was best and why, how to construct the perfect arrow, ten ways to impress your sister's friend, how to build the sturdiest and most effective slingshot, how to give yourself the perfect spray-on tan, what boys talk about when they're alone, written by an irritating girl named Bonnie who was two grades above him, or a companion piece about girls, written by the school's supposed ladies' man in the next grade up, with the tacky nickname Smoothie.

And while for Basil the end of World War II didn't mean much more than medals, crosses, and epaulettes, returning marines and victory parades, for Antonis Kambanis it was the end of a golden age of hand-over-fist profits, he knew things were about to change, the economy was booming, women had entered the workplace, the stock market was looking bullish, sales in off-the-rack clothes and shoes were taking off and it was only a matter of time, pitiless time, before his customers would decide his services weren't worth the leather he used to fix their shoes, and as Antonis bent over his bench hammering away at a heel, Basil looked sideways at him and wished with all his heart not to grow up to be like his father—and now it's three in the afternoon, the girls are still at school, Susan is in the bathroom, and Basil has set his mind on squashing a centipede that's hiding under the kitchen sink, but the harder he tries to corner it and whack it with the shoe he's taken off and is holding in his hand, the more deftly it slips away, seventeen pairs of poisonous legs, or maybe it's twenty, fluttering in unison as it plays hide-and-seek in the cracks and crevices of the wood, and Basil keeps pounding his shoe down without mercy, always too high, too low, too far to the right or left, and all he has to show for himself after seven unlucky attempts is a whole lot of nothing, and Susan is now standing behind him with that familiar withering look and a bath towel wrapped around her head like a turban, "What's gotten into you?" she asks, and Basil ignores her, preparing to land one final, deadly hit as soon as the centipede dares show itself again, and this time he manages to smush it with a loud slap on the wall, and Susan, who hasn't budged, asks him as he gets to his feet with the trophy in his hand if he's started dinner yet, or has he forgotten it's his turn to cook, and Basil, who really doesn't give a damn at this point, nods and smiles ironically, "Sure, of course," Susan insists, "Really? What?" and Basil waves his shoe triumphantly in the air as he says, "Centipede soup."

It was in fact his turn to make dinner, but he wasn't in the mood for much, so he pulled three identical sesame bagels out of the freezer and toasted them in the toaster, slathered them with cream cheese, dill, and smoked Atlantic salmon, garnished the plates with pickles and potato chips, and served them at the table with coleslaw and a liter of soda, and when Susan opened the front door and the girls came running into the house, Basil Kambanis grabbed his coat and keys and slipped out the back, got in the car and headed for the diner, his small earthly paradise which he'd soon have to sell for what felt like pocket money—while he dithered the offer had dropped by a whole ten thousand dollars, and Nino Cavani told him that soon there would be no demand at all, much less anything to negotiate, the market was stalled, the Federal Reserve wasn't printing new bills, and that damned Volcker kept raising rates to combat a stubborn, intractable inflation, how high could the fucking interest rates go, they were already at fifteen percent, unemployment was sky-high at eight percent, and worst of all, the papers and pundits saw no end in sight, and Basil kept tallying up his income and expenses in his head, the way things were going it would make more sense for him to keep the place closed, it'd be cheaper that way, less overhead, fewer taxes, and of course he'd save a fortune on gas if he weren't driving back and forth across the city every day, but as he arrived at the diner and saw it bizarrely full for the first time in months, on a Tuesday evening just before nightfall, he felt a kind of spiritual uplift, as if he'd made some mistake, there must be something he hadn't fully considered, hidden parameters, potential multipliers that hadn't been accounted for in the model he'd created, unknown numbers and factors that were now showing their blind obedience to an optimistic, deeply human plan.

The forty-two people who have filled his diner with their ready-made suits and pastel ties, their well-fed bellies and braying banter, all have something in common: they're all second- and third-generation Greek Americans who have come to town for the annual meeting of Chapter 69 of the American Hellenic Educational Progressive Association, or AHEPA, which is taking place in Camden, on the border of Dudley and Cramer Hill, for the first and perhaps last time in many years, on the glorious occasion of the sixty-fifth anniversary of the West Jersey chapter, which for over half that time had been based in Camden, until twenty-nine years and a few months ago when, after a stormy meeting and a dispute over taxes that lasted late into the night, the chapter had decided to follow so many of its sons of Pericles and daughters of Penelope, servants of Athena and acolytes of St. Thomas the Greek Orthodox protector, and moved from Mickle Street to resettle, after much toil and suffering, in the rapidly growing suburb of Cherry Hill. And here tonight are those very sons and daughters, all grown up with sons and daughters of their own, shining examples of Greek American achievement (emphasis on the American) who no longer have any reason to envy the other minorities who waltzed right in on earlier boats and set themselves up for success, claiming rights and primacy from their very birth, because the AHEPANs now speak perfect English, they've earned degrees, opened businesses, become lawyers and doctors and all have dreams, more or less shared, of one day seeing their children earn their first million, so they can crow over their young, fast-rising saplings—and so they can take pride in their dearly departed parents who made the difficult decision to uproot themselves and travel to the ends of the earth in hopes of a better life.

And now at the diner they keep ordering wine, beer, and ouzo from Lesvos that Basil keeps in a little closet for just such rare and special occasions, it's nearly ten and the diner is still packed, thick with smoke, wrapped in the soft warmth born of such unexpected, sweet, silky-smooth nights, and Veronica glides between the tables like a young girl, he can practically picture her in a cheerleader's uniform with pink bows in her hair, it's all bringing her back to the good old days when every evening felt like a party or celebration, the restaurants were always full and the streets buzzed with life, and Basil, having drunk a few glasses more than he should, starts chatting with a forty-year-old second-generation man with roots on Chios, a business consultant who plans on giving it all up and going back to the land of his forefathers, he's made enough money to last a lifetime, and now he'll go and spend it all on the island, restore the ruins of his family home, fill it with a family of his own, and whatever's left over he'll invest in a business plan bigger than anything the island has ever seen, the laws are favorable and things in Greece are changing, soon they'll have one of their own in the government, a democrat, a real stand-up guy raised in the States, a new sun is rising, brighter and more hopeful than ever, "Change here and now," he says, quoting Papandreou's slogan, now is their chance to return, now's the time to grab the bull by the horns, they have the know-how to alter the flow of history, to divert the river and nourish the dry land, to revive the dying peripheries, and he bangs his fist on the table with anger and longing for all the things he believes are his by right, passed down from grandfather to father to grandson time and again, a distant inheritance that traveled from mouth to mouth, generation to generation—"Fuck it, what's everyone waiting for?"—and Basil feels like he can't sit still in his seat, and as he swivels on the stool and the words of the guy from Chios pummel him from all sides, the solution comes to him like lightning splitting the dark, or like a star whose light has been traveling through the sky for thousands of years and suddenly shines full and resplendent before him: his Greek might be broken, his finances shipwrecked, but the dollar is strong and the drachma weak, the exchange rate holding steady at 43 drachmas per dollar, an advantage that, if properly calculated and wisely invested, could bring back all the lost profits of his life, all the things his run of bad luck has scattered to the winds, to hell with Susan and the girls, the proceeds from the sale of the diner should be his, and suddenly out of the dark haze of drink he sees a leisurely, light-hearted future emerge, an eternal summer sunk in the hum of crickets and soft plashing of waves, and he can almost taste the chervil on his tongue, paired on his plate with sweet green peas and freshly cleaned artichokes.

The next morning, in the first weak, creeping light of February, 1981, Basil Kambanis wakes up on the leather sofa inside the door of his diner, he slept awkwardly and his right shoulder is aching, his head feels leaden, the Ariadne looks like a tornado passed through, and as he gets up to make himself coffee and splash some water on his face, the previous night comes spinning back at him like a whirlpool or turbine, and he grabs a broom and mop to get a head start on the woman who comes in to clean every morning, and as he's tidying and sweeping up the worst of the mess, a group of young Hispanics with ski masks and hoodies pass by the diner window, and a skinny little guy, a bundle of nerves and attitude, stops short, hikes up his pants, which are two sizes too big, and peers in through the window, weighing a large stone in his hand.

X

thanksgiving dinner:
placing the baby's high chair
in the empty space
NICK VIRGILIO

Antonis Kambanis didn't intend to fall in love, in fact he'd long since resigned himself to the likelihood of breathing his last breath with no one at his side, closing his own eyes in death, helpless and heirless, in a small bachelor pad with a back garden, and if he had any money to his name when he died, he'd leave it to a charity for cancer patients to exorcise the bad hand he'd been dealt, because after all he'd been through he still believed in fate, just as his mother had, and before her a long line of luckless progenitors who had known only poverty and sickness—so when his business partner finally wore him down and convinced him to go to the annual AHEPA ball at the luxurious Walt Whitman Hotel, Antonis Kambanis pulled his old, moth-eaten suit out of his closet and tried it on, only to realize to his great sorrow that it had been nearly eleven years since his mother's death and he'd gained twice as many pounds, the trouser legs were a smidge too short and the jacket wouldn't button, there was no way he could show up at a fancy ball in that awful getup, and he chickened out and sent word to his partner not to expect him, he was sick, his whole body ached, he was burning with fever, but Takis knew him well, knew how timid he was and wouldn't take no for an answer, and when he discovered the root of the problem, he sent their Levantine seamstress with a borrowed suit to clean him up as much as she could in the time they had—and this, at a quarter past eight on April 22, 1933, Antonis Kambanis stood before the mirror in his house looking unexpectedly well-dressed.

For the Greek American community, after the holy days of Easter, the annual ball was undoubtedly the event of the year, everyone and his brother was always enthusiastically present, and in the weeks leading up to the event, regardless of financial hardships, old gowns and suits would be taken apart and sewn anew in keeping with the latest styles, which is why, unbeknownst to himself, Antonis Kambanis enjoyed a silent general appreciation, since many dresses and even more suits had been given new life at his little shop: the seamstress had hands of gold, she was commonly described as "Rockefeller with a needle," in fact rumor had it that even some high-society ladies who had fallen on hard times made use of her services, they would slip in right before closing to entrust her with their gaudy, flashy possessions, expensive gowns that over the years had started to sag and fade and were crying out to be mended, updated, given a new lease on life—and at the ball, while his Salonican partner gazed in admiration at the Levantine seamstress's flounces and double stitches, dazed by the frills and frippery, the sweet, intoxicating perfumes, Antonis Kambanis stood in a corner and watched indifferently as the band came out onto the stage and started to play Greek foxtrots and tangos, and while the sultry singer belted out recent hits about new loves, or mournful refrains about times now lost but not forgotten, Kambanis fiddled with the well-worn baptismal cross around his neck, which he had never once taken off in all his thirty-two years.

And then he saw her, upright and alone in the crowd, carrying a little donation basket, and a minute later there she was again, spinning gracefully through the room, laughing with a pack of classy men, while their wives, on the margins of the circle and the conversation, threw her poisonous looks full of hatred and rage, and Antonis Kambanis gathered his courage and went up to her, dropped some bills in her basket for the erection of a Greek Orthodox church, and began speaking to her shyly, she was nearly ten years his senior, and beautiful, with noble features, slightly hardened around the edges by her age and some rocky times, but still striking, with remarkable, hypnotizing hazel eyes, and Antonis was so awkward around women and ignorant of their ways that when she looked him deep in the eye, he was so startled that he went to pull out more money to toss into the basket, and she laughed, naturally and impulsively, and grabbed his hand to stop him. "Enough," she said, those first dollars were plenty to bless the cause, and then she introduced herself, "I'm Rallou, from Mytilini," and they shook hands, "Antonis, Antonis Kambanis," and with a girlish twirl and a happy, ringing, gurgling laugh, she vanished from sight, only to reappear three or four groups further down, arm in arm with a girlfriend from Smyrna, the basket tucked under her arm—and just then, as if it had been agreed ahead of time, as the clock struck midnight the partygoers set all the charity work and philanthropy of the previous day aside, signaling to the band that it was time to start dancing in earnest.

He needed to talk to her again, and as the hour grew later that need became torturous, possessing him almost physically, and he kept looking for ways to get close to her, but though he was wiry and spry, the poor sap had no grace at all, no idea how to dance, and so he stood in a corner like a stump waiting for the moment when she might twirl back to his side so he could cast out a few words of admiration to reel her in, but the few times he saw her headed in his direction, the opportunity slipped through his fingers like oil, someone else called to her, or a girlfriend waved her over, and Antonis sat there like a cat on hot bricks, until the clock showed a quarter past two and he finally decided that he didn't have the guts to approach her again and left his post and headed for the bathroom, patiently waiting his turn while the band played slow songs and mournful amanedes, and then all of a sudden he saw her, recognized her silhouette behind the frosted glass of the door as she stood at the sink, water caressing her hands, and he lurched forward into the bathroom like a battering ram to recite the few sentences he'd cobbled together and had been whispering to himself for hours, only the words had climbed to the edge of his lips, turned around, and were thumbing their noses at him, balancing between inside and out, flatly refusing to take a step forward into the light so he could say his piece and be done with it for heaven's sake, and since his tongue wouldn't obey, his hands took over and did what not even a thousand words could have done: he took the little tin cross from around his neck and passed it over her head, and Rallou lowered her eyes, thoroughly moved, submissive before the man who had crowned her queen of his home, his future wife.

Rallou's only wealth was her gaiety and good looks, she was like the morning dew that revives the leaves on plants and gives their stamens a fresh coat of gloss, and she willingly gave in to Antonis Kambanis's desire because he was different, shy but capable, good with his hands—qualities others considered weaknesses of character, Rallou interpreted as discretion and respect, and in October 1933 they set off together into the uncharted waters of marriage, making a common home in Kambanis's little house, where there was plenty of room for them both, and in the beginning they would head to the shop together, too, and everything ticked along as smoothly as clockwork. The only one who didn't take kindly to this new presence was Antonis's partner Takis, who was annoyed to find that the icon of St. Demetrios on his horse, patron saint of his hometown of Salonica, had been moved to a different wall, with a needlepoint from Mytilini now hanging in its place, and he was bothered by the misplaced awl, the crumbs he found strewn now and again over the workbench and floor, and he felt himself getting hot under the collar, sometimes he even wanted to throw up his hands, cash in his share and quit, because he was excitable, temperamental, and a misogynist to boot, and he found himself lighting one cigarette after the next to calm his nerves and soothe his secret longing for Rallou, whom he himself had fallen for years before, though she had never paid him the slightest attention, and here she was now, the stupid skirt, acting like a second boss, a nuisance and a bother right there in his shop.

The heavy weather at Second Chance showed no sign of letting up, it was as if a north wind had blown through, turning everything upside down, and there was no sign of a cleansing rain that might wash away the mumbling and complaints that had settled like dust over everything, dulling the surfaces until you could no longer see what things were made of or how resilient they actually were, and since all Antonis cared about was how business was going and his share of the profits, Takis kept his mouth shut about all the things going amiss and awry, though they rattled him deeply, and he simply let his poison out at a slow drip, in malicious comments, muttered jabs and snipes, becoming so unbearably unpleasant that only a snapping retort from Rallou could put him in his place, and so, bit by bit, day by day, week by week, an unhealthy pattern was established at the shop, which at first surprised their regular customers with its relentless drive, but over time became rather quaint, an odd kind of entertainment feature, Takis ribbing and belittling Rallou, and Rallou winging compliments right back at him that would make even the toughest of men redden with rage and shame—and whenever Antonis tried to restore some kind of balance, he only got in the way of their friendly fire, and so eventually he learned his lesson and withdrew, letting them rage as much as they liked and turning even more concertedly to his work, with such talent and vigor that, just short of two years later, they were able to open their first branch, in Parkside.

A new era was dawning. The 21st amendment lifting prohibition in December 1933 marked the end of the chemists' war that the Coolidge administration had waged on tipplers since the winter of 1926, by denaturing alcohol with methyl alcohol, gasoline, and formaldehyde, costing the lives of thousands of Americans who unwittingly consumed a blue-tinged whisky whose chemical base was intended for the industrial production of paint and fuel, and in the absence of ethanol, mobsters liberated whole batches of the stuff from warehouses and factories and flooded the market with toxic poisons, falsely assuring customers that it was good stuff, top-shelf, straight from the source—and Antonis Kambanis, who in his youth had distributed entire cases of that supposedly top-shelf booze in a hearse named Gina, would during those final days of 1933 recall every so often that poisonous grappa that could revive even the dead, and would feel a small, bitter sorrow that burned going down, and then he'd shake it off and think instead of the fine, generous days he was living, and imagine even better days to come, as he stacked dollar bills in a chest for the son who would surely soon make his appearance, because the day he stepped onto the boat that would take him away from his native island he'd promised his mother that when he got married and his wife gave birth to their first son, he would name him after his dearly departed father, Vassilis. His child would be a son, and that would be his name, Vassilis, because he had promised, he had given his word.

But the stronger Antonis Kambanis's desire grew for a sturdy, healthy son who would eventually take over the reins of his booming business, the more conception seemed to hover just out of reach, as if God were upset with him for some reason and had dug in His divine heels. There were mornings when Kambanis looked with suspicion at Rallou's steadfastly slender form, as if the secret of fecundity was hiding in that abyss of femininity and resourcefulness, and he kept measuring it with his eye, but instead of getting plump, Rallou seemed on the contrary to be losing weight, until one day he asked her straight out if perhaps she might not be fertile and they were just wasting their time, and Rallou pulled her dress up, her panties down, and spat straight in his face, how dare he, her body was graced with the secrets of the garden of Eden and the opulence of the East, the problem was his small, shriveled dick, and Antonis Kambanis raised his hand and hit her hard, once, twice, three times in a row, and then his rage died down and his fury subsided and he locked himself in the bathroom to take a few sharp breaths, and three weeks later, once the bruises had faded, he apologized, and to prove he meant it, he rented a car and driver and took her to a movie at the drive-in that had opened in the eastern suburb of Pennsauken along the Cooper River, and they sat there in silence in the thick darkness and watched *Wives Beware*, starring the forty-year-old, ever-dapper, dressed-to-the-nines Adolphe Menjou.

From that moment, for all the years that the sexual act persisted, once in a blue moon, between Antonis and Rallou Kambanis, it was a bloodthirsty, covert battle, out of which no victor ever emerged, only two battered creatures, exhausted by the conflict and wounded by the stinging words, and when Antonis was in a dark mood, he would raise his hand against her with the same impulse and rage as that first time, and Rallou, who over time became used to her peculiar conjugal obligations, would dress him up and down with all kinds of shameful names, and thus in the privacy of their home they moved together through moments of minor and major tumult, as the months passed slowly and torturously, while at work Takis's sharpness had dulled, he was always forgetting things, dates and appointments, and Antonis was overwhelmed with orders, numbers, and accounts, and Rallou, purely out of spite, was less and less willing to contribute, to provide any kind of assistance, to carry out any task at all, no matter how minor in size or scale.

And while President Roosevelt was serving his first term in the White House vigorously proclaiming the New Deal, promising well-paying jobs and opportunities for all, Rallou was slowly discovering the salutary and healing properties of drink, specifically ouzo, which if you downed it on an empty stomach would quickly numb your head and lighten your heart, and as FDR fought tooth and nail to keep his disability from polio—which had cost him two strong legs and nearly his political career—out of the newspapers, Rallou began to drink openly, glass after glass, evening after evening, and then in the afternoons, too, and one winter night when the roads were slick with ice, Antonis Kambanis, whose days had been entirely absorbed by the prospect of expanding operations into neighboring Philadelphia, fell into bed an hour earlier than usual, mulling over their annual budget and crossing himself as he counted the long line of zeros that had filled his pockets to bursting, then turned and looked out the window and saw Rallou's thin figure crossing the street, staggering, a worn jacket over her shoulders and a paper bag from the grocer under her arm, and he fell headlong in love with her all over again, with a tenderness that reminded him how much he too had suffered over the years, and he felt a sudden need to support her in her downhill turn, and he hurried to the door and took her urgently into his arms and all night whispered sweet nothings and promised her white elephants and pink castles in the air, told her that things would be different from then on, starting the very next day, things had to change, because it was now just a matter of time—three months, seven days, and a few hours, to be precise—until something came to alter their lives forever.

XI

the old neighborhood
falling to the wrecking ball:
names in the sidewalks
NICK VIRGILIO

Pete weighed the rock in his hand. It had taken him two weeks to figure out where his sister was hiding and he was almost certain she was cooking up some kind of trouble for him, they'd never gotten along, he never even really liked their mother, she tried, the poor fool, but he couldn't stand her small-mindedness, how she just gave up, let poverty and misery walk all over her, and it came out in hysterics and greasy smacks, whereas look at him, he'd already saved up a nice wad of cash from manning the corner and helping move stolen cars and stereos, he made more in a week than that stupid Louisa got from welfare in three whole months—and just then he was hyped up on weed laced with cocaine, his mind making crazy, unlikely connections, jumping from thought to thought with such speed and precision that all his senses seemed electrified, nothing escaped him, he was on top of the world, all set to become a true Quiñón, and after that a king, and as he felt the sharp warmth of the rock in his hand, he whistled to the two other guys from the gang, and on cue they all leaned their bodies back together like synchronized bows to gather force and speed, then threw their rocks in unison, fractions of a second apart, and as the plate-glass window of the diner cracked and shattered along the length of the sidewalk, Pete raised the borrowed revolver and delivered a final blow, a first and last shot, to the corner of the window that was still standing, and shouted, "Say hi to my little sister," and the three of them started running, cackling with laughter, teasing and shoving one another, then piled into a parked car, swerved a 180 as one of the guys raised a middle finger out the window, a move lifted straight from a gangster film, and disappeared, gunning the engine down the empty avenue.

Basil Kambanis is distraught, in all his years in Camden he's never felt threatened, and if he ever happened to worry it was only a fleeting feeling, the suspicion of a bad turn that never materialized, the shadow of a danger that passed right by but never touched him, bad things always happened to other people, who, in his humble opinion, were either asking for it, or were too bold and reckless, giving disaster fertile ground to flourish. But now his hands are trembling and Miranda, the Colombian woman who cleans the place in the mornings, makes him sit down on the leather couch so the police officer can start to take his statement as she goes to call Susan, who appears shortly after—and now the officer closes his notebook, Miranda is sweeping up the broken glass, and Susan is talking to the workers who came to measure the windows and take the order, fortunately the insurance will cover the damage, it seems to have been an attempted robbery that got offtrack, it's strange they didn't try to make off with the money in the register, maybe they'd been staking the place out, or had shouted some warning, but Basil insists that they didn't say anything, or at least nothing he could really make out, one kid shouted something that from a distance sounded to him like "Say hi to the little shitter," and the second officer shakes his head and puts his hand over his mouth to cover a yawn, it was clearly just some junkies out for fun, unless he'd had a prior run-in with some gang and they had a mark on him, "No," Susan answers, "No," Basil confirms, and the incident is recorded in a police report that will soon enter the byzantine archives of the department downtown, and the patrol car rolls off toward more fertile grounds, Leto and Minnie are at home doing their homework together, the workers will come that afternoon to install the new windows, "Are you going to stay here and wait for them?" Susan asks, and Basil looks at his clenched fists, which are still shaking, and says "I'm thinking of giving it all up and moving to Greece, I want you to come with me," and Susan meets his eye and wants to shout "What's wrong with you?" but keeps quiet, bites her tongue, then leaps up from her seat like a spring, tossing him a few crumbs of compassion: "I'll think it over and we'll talk."

Susan thinks it over, it doesn't take long, the time it takes to get in the car and drive home, and since traffic is light at that time of day the whole business troubles her, or rather annoys her, for fifteen minutes at most, she has no intention whatsoever of setting up shop in a country whose language she doesn't speak, a country that just six years earlier emerged from a seven-year dictatorship, a country that always makes her think of the bleak news from Latin America, Argentina, or Chile, no way, she'll stay in Camden, or if she has to she'll move to Vermont, she's always wanted to live there, she's heard it's the East Coast version of the old, hippie San Francisco, the schools are good, the state politics are progressive, and with the money she'd get from Basil she could build a little cabin in the woods close to some small town, someplace like Jericho, or could rent an apartment in Burlington until she decided on her next steps, maybe she'd start a farm growing organic produce or a little shop selling restored antiques she'd buy at seasonal bazaars and garage sales, and the more she thinks about it, the more hopeful she feels, maybe divorce is a necessary evil that will unjam her life, a narrow, overlooked, one-way street that will lead her out onto a quiet dirt road with no police officers, traffic lights, or street signs, and for a while, as long as the ride lasts, she'll do whatever she wants, go wherever she pleases, there'll be no one looking over her shoulder—but then she gets out of the car, walks up to the house, opens the front door, and sees the living room looking like a battlefield, Leto has shoved the sofa and glass coffee table aside and set Minnie up like a Subbuteo goalkeeper between two dining room chairs, and at the precise moment Susan walks in she kicks the ball, which hits the chair, knocks it over, bounces off the wall, ricochets into a porcelain vase, and slides into the goal, and Susan realizes once and for all that she isn't alone, that this one-way street may in fact turn into a dirt road full of bumps and potholes, and she'll be dragging around these two ramped-up bumper cars who keep flying off in all directions, following their own intransigent rules, and who would prefer, ideally right this instant, to stop at a playground or maybe a dirty, muddy race track perfect for drag racing and stunts—and with that thought she collapses exhausted onto the cockeyed sofa, letting her body slowly adjust to this new, anarchic, inconvenient arrangement.

Leto has always been a difficult child with a predisposition for trouble, a defiant streak, a tendency to get into scrapes, a true talent for springing up in unexpected places, running you ragged, and wreaking havoc of all kinds, some accidental and some entirely vindictive, like the time Susan had scolded her for spilling honey on the kitchen floor and Leto had trampled in it, smeared it around, and then tracked it all over the house, making a beeline for their new leather sofa and climbing up with her honey-covered shoes, and when Susan started shouting and even slapped her, enraged by the chaos the little girl had created, five-year-old Leto snuck a pair of scissors into her parents' room and shredded the black dress her mother had set aside, washed and ironed, to wear that afternoon to an interview for a desk job at a small but upcoming publishing house, and then, beaming with pride, presented the tattered strips of cloth to Susan as an abstract, avant-garde artwork she called "lots of dresses for mommy," pushing Susan to hysterics, even to the edge of a stroke—it was all Basil could do to restrain her, to calm her down and keep her from making things worse, ordering the girl to go to her room and not come out until her mother was calm, and Leto obeyed right away, somehow Basil always managed things with Leto so much better than Susan, mostly because he bribed her on the sly with toys and baubles to get her to sit still and listen, until one day Leto requested her first dollar in payment for good behavior and all hell broke loose, she got the first real spanking of her life, though of course it made no difference on the inside, she just realized at the calculating age of seven that it was better to keep her wants and desires to herself, letting them surface only occasionally, like pearls sealed tightly in their shells, which we open to show others only in hopes that they'll hand them joyfully back, ideally accompanied by a fine gold chain.

And though her parents annoyed her, she still loved them, because together they were the one and only unshakeable, solid thing in her life, her safe place, along with soccer, of course, and when she was having a tough time at school, or getting taunted by the boys in her grade, who were thrown off not only by her stupid, unpronounceable name, but by her early, awkward development, or when the girls called her by that dumb 68, surrounding her in a cloud of giggles and hints—"practically 69"—and

her teachers pretended not to notice, entirely indifferent to what she was going through, Leto would
feel the anger and injustice suffocating her, the
earth quaking beneath her feet, and at the smallest
pretext she would lash out at her parents to let off
steam, and once she'd calmed down what always
surprised her the most was how they never held any
of it against her, the day after a fight the air had always cleared and everything was business as usual.
There was one time when she almost screwed up for
real, a stupid rainy Wednesday when the drains
were clogged and the schoolyard practically flooded
and she went and picked a fight with a boy who had
insulted her in front of her entire geometry class,
they'd been arguing about which basketball team
was best that year and he called her a clueless lanky
lesbian, she didn't give a shit that he'd called her a
lesbian, because she wasn't, she had the hots for
the gym teacher, a half-Italian hunk who was killer
at soccer too, even played for the amateur Ravens,
and she didn't care that he'd called her lanky, because it was true, she was tall, and there wasn't a
thing she could do to about that—but being called
clueless was totally unfair, and it was the last straw,
and when the drains finally overflowed during recess and filthy water rushed out over the cement,
Leto put the boy in a headlock and pulled him facedown to the ground, whispering through gritted
teeth for him to take it all back, and she'd been entirely prepared to drown him in that disgusting
water, and might have done it if the teacher on recess duty hadn't seen them, pulled them apart,
given them both a two-day suspension, and called

their guardians to come pick them up, and Basil, who rushed straight to the school, heard the whole story from a teary, sensitive, fragile boy in the same class as Leto who was hoping for revenge against his bullying classmates, and so Basil didn't hesitate to give the principal and the teacher who had witnessed the fight a piece of his mind, and on the way home with Leto he didn't raise the subject, in fact he didn't speak at all, and it was Susan, on the second day of the suspension, while she was grudgingly tidying the house, running a dust cloth over the furniture, who suggested to her daughter, who was lying perfectly still with her beat-up sneakers on the arm of the sofa, if in addition to soccer she might be interested in taking a dance class together at the Dudley civic center, and Leto shook her head and, without thinking twice, blurted out what the gym teacher always said to the two effeminate, friendless boys in her class, "Dancing is for sissies," though the gym teacher didn't leave it at that but always yelled, "Come on, dolls, let's see you run, leave the pliés and pirouettes for home," pointing to Leto as a shining example who always made him look good, coming in twenty yards ahead of the rest of the class when they sprinted, "Good job, thatta girl, good job, Leto, you're a star," he would shout, and she would run even faster, flying down the track, because she was crazy in love and wanted to please him more than anything else in the world.

Minnie bends down to gather the pieces of the broken vase that lie scattered over the floor while Leto kicks the ball into the corner of the sofa, it was a beautiful vase, Susan had bought it in the spring of 1970 on a whirlwind trip to Rhinebeck one gorgeous weekend, with a carefree Leto toddling around in drooping, shit-filled diapers and Basil delighted at having discovered the perfect blackberry jam, and now Minnie picks up the biggest pieces, trying to fit them together, to see how bad the damage is, whether the vanished image of that formerly solid object might somehow be restored, and bit by bit the outlines and shading come together, but a few key pieces are missing, and some tiny shards that went flying and are now lost on the floor, and as her fingers dig around for them in the rug, they instead find a bit of trash, a hair, some dust, and a pebble, and Minnie wonders if what she's dredged up could shape another vase, a makeshift imitation of the original that might still resemble it in some ways, if she could heal its wounds with a little dust, a few hairs, some stones from the yard, and perhaps in the end something neither partial nor ugly might emerge—and then, as Leto keeps kicking the ball into the corner of the sofa, because she wants to say she's sorry but can't, Susan stands up, takes the broken pieces from Minnie's hands and throws them in the garbage, because she doesn't have the time, the patience, or the energy for any more emotional outbursts, the vase is broken and where it belongs now is in the trash.

Basil Kambanis stands behind the new plate glass window the workers have just installed, observing it; there's something about it that bothers him, doesn't sit well, he's annoyed by this gleaming revival of something that's already set to expire, just a while ago Nino Cavani called to report that a better offer came in, two thousand above the last, and he shouldn't be stupid, they should close the deal and shake on it today, Basil asked for some time to think it over and Cavani gave him a hard time, but in the end let him have another few hours to make his decision, stressing in no uncertain terms that if the answer was no, Basil shouldn't count on working with him anymore, there won't ever be a better offer, end of story, and he's not going to waste his time on a hopeless case, and Basil looks at his watch, thinking how any minute now the stay on his execution will expire, and he looks at the spotless, utterly flawless window and feels the ticking second hand on his watch suffocating him as the phone in the diner rings, and he feels just like he felt on his very first day of kindergarten, when he refused to go inside, just stood there thunderstruck in the yard and watched as his mother walked away, and when she turned her head and saw him, feet glued to the pavement, she suddenly whirled around, ran straight toward him, and slapped him in front of his new classmates, then dragged him by the ear into the school, and Basil goes to lift the receiver but can't, something won't let him, and for a moment, a few ticks of the watch, his fingers hang there in the air, kneading the emptiness before them as if they could tame it, trying to imprison a handful of air.

XII

Only themselves understand themselves, and the likes
    of themselves,
As Souls only understand Souls.
WALT WHITMAN

Rallou's pregnancy came out of nowhere, a bolt from
the blue. Antonis Kambanis tried to remember how
and when she might have conceived, counting the
weeks and days and trying to make it all fit on the
calendar, he had a faint memory but wasn't quite
sure, kept looking at her sideways, and whenever
his hand started to itch and he went to raise it, he
thought twice and shoved it back in his pocket, the
child was his, there was no doubt about it, and if a
few small slaps happened to escape him during a
minor quarrel they were simply passing clouds,
marital caresses, at the end of the day he was the
pillar, the infallible man of the house, and he
worked hard to make sure she had everything she
needed, there was always ice in the house, fruit and
meat and vegetables, and he'd bring little presents,

hand-sewn baby clothes, tiny outfits, and Rallou, who had only gained five or six pounds in four months, felt as if she'd been forced to swallow a stone, which had settled in her stomach and put out roots that burrowed into her guts, splitting her open, and the more ouzo she downed, the heavier the stone grew and the more roots it sprouted, seemingly out of spite, and at first she couldn't tell whether the stone or the drink was making her vomit, and then she stopped thinking altogether, made up her mind that she was carrying a stone, a *petra*, and when she was drunk she would tell the baby she would call it Petros, it would be their secret, Petros from *petra*, the millstone around her neck—and in her drunken haze she would croon crude songs to it, then fall into a deep sleep and dream of steep canyons falling from bloody heights, and down below butchered newborn calves wrapped in transparent, airtight bags.

And that's just how their Vassilis emerged from her womb, drenched in blood and amniotic fluid, and for a moment she thought his cry was some primitive vestige of her own body or self, and only when the scissors cut the umbilical cord did Rallou take a deep breath, turn over on her side, and grow calm, and she knew deep down that there was no sense trying to change her fate, she wouldn't ever love that boy, what she had brought into the world was nothing short of a prison sentence, a condemnation, and soon enough that condemnation would begin to grow, would acquire a voice and substance and judgment, and when they put him in her arms to nurse, her eyes darkened and her hands pushed the infant away from her aching nipple, and the head nurse ran to grab the baby out of her arms, something in the woman's eyes frightened her, and she asked one of the nurses to call the doctor right away, and Rallou lay there staring at the bright white ceiling and didn't speak to another human for forty days. During her weeks of mourning when she was stuck at home with the baby, she would shove a bottle in his mouth to keep him from crying, she never nursed him, and though the doctor had advised Antonis to keep an eye on his wife and child, Antonis was sure things would settle down over time and didn't take that advice seriously, and while he was going about his business at home and at the shop, Rallou's hatred deepened like cracks in a building that undermine its strength and resistance, and when the smallest shudder of an earthquake comes along it shakes the foundations, putting the whole structure in danger. Rallou emptied carafe after carafe until she could barely stand, another sip and she would collapse, and beside her in his crib her six-month-old baby cried, screamed, and flailed, the doctor had told them he'd be cutting his first teeth any time now, and Rallou leaned against the baby's crib, poured ouzo to the brim of his bottle, and dropped it into the crib, and the baby sucked at the bottle, settled down, and finally shut its wailing mouth.

Antonis Kambanis knew that his wife often had a few drinks, though of course he had no idea the extent of it, they had agreed on two small bottles a week, but Rallou got her hands on much more than that from a Greek grocer, a distant cousin from the same village and a tippler himself, they were bound by ties of blood and he didn't have the heart to say no, and of course he too knew the irresistible enticements of alcohol, and on afternoons or evenings when she was out of money and the drink had run dry, he would send his errand boy with a watered-down carafe or two on the house or a demijohn of second-rate retsina, something to help soften her sorrows, a comforting smell and taste to take the sting out of her family troubles and the routines of married life. The only thing Rallou did well and with a fairly conscious mind was the cooking, and despite her frequent drunkenness, her hands knew their way around the kitchen, she was an ace, a first-rate cook, her sauces always came out perfectly, the smell of her roasts and casseroles filled the house with their mouthwatering warmth —she had an incredible talent, which of course was wasted in that small house, and as long as there was a plate of home-cooked food waiting for him each night, Antonis Kambanis never noticed how deep her need was, how serious her problem, and only little Vassilis, still too young to talk, sensed his mother's undying hatred haunting him and the house and lived the daily nightmare of her drinking, as the smell of alcohol filled the room and seeped into the walls, leaving a bittersweet taste that dried out his mouth and turned his stomach. He was afraid of his mother and rarely approached her, and mostly avoided his father, too, because Antonis was quick to anger and had an awkward way about him, and so Vassilis took comfort in made-up stories, in invisible superheroes who lived in the cushions of the sofa and watched over him, on a secret mission to protect him from any harm.

And that harm always came in small doses, there was never any blustering rage, it just wrapped itself around you slowly and subtly, almost gently, so you got used to it, considered it almost normal, and of course it never left permanent marks, just a few scratches and bruises that changed color and shape like the seasons, a caress with his father's belt, a slap with the underside of his mother's slipper, and the constant, steady swearing about a broken plate, a dirty glass, melted ice, a tap left running, food uneaten on a plate—and so Vassilis's first childish words didn't come to name or define objects, but to accompany and baptize the small, malevolent, vindictive acts that had a cumulative power, that piled up, that fitted themselves together like the tiles of a hateful, hideous mosaic depicting a holy family that seemed always incomplete, a mosaic presided over by slender, austere shapes, marionettes of kindness who had no voice to ask forgiveness, just fiery eyes out for revenge.

At three years old Vassilis Kambanis could still barely put two words together, his development was slow and torturous, and Antonis Kambanis, impatient to teach him all the things an only son needed to know, never got any response to his evening lectures apart from a brief searching glance that soon fell to the ground, landing on a pair of tiny saddle shoes: little Vassilis Kambanis's favorite hobby was tying and untying his shoelaces, he could keep himself busy for hours on end making loose bows and knots, it was his way of taking up as little space as possible—as he sat there quietly playing with his laces Rallou forgot all about him, and Antonis did, too, they were hypnotized by the rhythm of that tying and untying, the silent repetition of that meaningless act—and then one weekday morning, on one of the few times when Antonis brought his son to the shop to get him used to the tools and the space, Father Stelios came in and asked in his slow Serres drawl to have his best pair of shoes spruced up for his eldest daughter's wedding that Saturday, and as the priest glanced around the shop his eyes fell on the child, and he asked what his name was, then asked a second and third and fourth time, and his beard was long and gray and his eyes dark and frightening, seeking the one and only truth, and Vassilis began to cry and right there on the spot pronounced the first complete sentence of his life.

If the United States officially entered the Second World War after the bombing of Pearl Harbor on December 7, 1941, in the Kambanis household the hand-to-hand combat began a week earlier, with the revelation that Vassilis Kambanis answered not to Vassilis but to Petros, a name his mother had been calling him since he was still in the womb, Petros after *petra*, her millstone, and during the whole walk home from the shop in Parkside to the house on the border of Dudley and Cramer Hill Antonis Kambanis kept asking the boy what his name was, and he kept tearfully insisting that his name was Petros, and the blows rained down until the boy's cheeks were covered in purple splotches, and when they finally got home and a drunk Rallou came to the door, Antonis Kambanis didn't hold back, started smashing and throwing anything close at hand, turned the place upside-down, then grabbed Rallou by the hair and the boy by the collar, dragged them around the living room, and told them to get it into their thick skulls that there was no Petros in that house and never would be, there was a great and powerful Antonis, and a Vassilis named for his grandfather who could squeeze water out of stones, and a stupid alcoholic mother who drank so much she couldn't even remember her own child's name, God damn the moment he picked her out of the crowd.

It took two days for Rallou to recover—not so much from the beating, compared to other times it hadn't been bad, a few scratches and bruises and a scrape on her back from the door jamb, but because the next morning young Vassilis Kambanis finally found his voice, as if whatever had tied up his tongue had suddenly come loose and he had magically, unexpectedly found the words to articulate his train of thought, producing his first intelligible phrases in perfectly accented American English— after all, the little tyke was a native of this country, and he now carried himself a bit more proudly, standing a bit taller, drawing a dividing line between himself and his parents. His declaration of independence had begun with his first articulation of language, his first speech act, and in his mouth the name Vassilis soon became Basil, because he wasn't Greek, didn't feel Greek, had no real ties to his poor, parched ancestral lands, his parents with their heavy accents and awkward manners embarrassed him, he never wanted to be seen with them out in the street, and at school Basil was a name people could understand, it rolled off the tongue, had a pleasing roundness and energy, and though his father tried to convince him at least to go by Vassilis at home, Basil Kambanis refused to negotiate his inalienable right to self-definition, he was the boss, master, and caretaker of his name, and early on he decided that Vassilis wasn't to his liking, so to the customary question "What's your name, son?" repeated ad nauseum by acquaintances, strangers, and passersby, he would always answer "Basil"—his name was Basil, end of story, and no matter what happened, he wouldn't change it for anything or anyone. Rallou had brought an American citizen into the world who stubbornly refused to speak the language of his forebears, and though he understood everything they said, he always responded in English, and even pointedly corrected their grammar and pronunciation.

Antonis Kambanis, meanwhile, had gotten a bit heavier in both body and mood and had acquired the bad habit of stopping off every few days at the Niagara coffee house on his way home to play a game of cards, nurse his wine, and chat with the other regulars and with the owner, a guy named Mikis from Edessa, about the war raging in the West and East, the brutal German occupation of Greece, America's open fronts in Asia and the Pacific, and everyone added their two cents, talking about forces and strategy, what their odds were with the Allies, if the British could stop the Germans in North Africa, at El Alamein, or if the Russians could halt them at Stalingrad. Heated debates on these topics flew back and forth all day and all night in shops, homes, and streets throughout the city, Camden's experience of the war may have been indirect but it still felt active, with thirty thousand of its women and men working at Antonis's former place of employment, the New York Shipbuilding Corporation, whose shipyard on the eastern shore of the Delaware River was feeding the war with the biggest global production of warships, navy vessels, transport ships, and destroyers. Antonis had once even caught a distant glimpse of the USS *Indianapolis* on its maiden voyage nearly a decade before it was sunk in Pearl Harbor, and he'd seen the passenger ships known as the 4 Aces, built for cruise lines servicing the Mediterranean, until they were requisitioned for the war and all but one lost to enemy action. The one that survived, orphaned by all its siblings, was the exotically named *Exochorda*, nickname "the Bride," which as part of the war effort had been renamed, regendered, and given a new identity as the military transport ship the USS *Harry Lee*, and went down in the annals of World War II as a trigger-happy fighter whose glowing career won it seven stars for bravery in battle. Antonis Kambanis had once given another kind of star to his future wife, just a few days before their wedding, it was dry and smelled strongly of anise, and Rallou laughed, took it, gave him a mock military salute, and fixed it with a safety pin to the lapel of her jacket. They were allies in the battle of marriage, allies who, when there was no one and nothing left to fight, resorted to not-so-friendly fire—until one night, as Antonis Kambanis left the Niagara coffee house after midnight and turned the corner heading home, three men in nearly identical dark suits and trench coats pushed him down, grabbed him by both arms, and shuffled him straight into a pitch-black luxury Ford.

XIII

the cathedral bell
is shaking a few snowflakes
from the morning air
NICK VIRGILIO

Basil Kambanis has been sitting in the car for an hour with the motor and lights off two blocks from his house, with a Bank of America check in his pocket that renders him the sole beneficiary of the laughable sum of twenty-three thousand dollars, and it's not that he regrets selling the restaurant at a bargain price, he's been wanting to unload it for years, to shake free of the overwhelming responsibilities and endless bills, but he'd imagined it all so differently, he thought he'd have some kind of plan for his next steps, some sure thing to turn to the morning after the sale, and he'd dreamed so often of the day when he'd finally get to linger in bed, certain that his decision would bring him instant returns, that his prospects had been traded in for dollars that would now begin to multiply as soon as he put his brilliant new scheme into action—and yet the unfortunate truth was that Basil Kambanis hadn't made any plan at all, shining or dull, back-lit or front-lit, all he had were a few vague possibilities knocking around in his head that he had trouble squeezing into a mold, shaping into something permanent or even halfway solid. He liked cars, but not enough to open a used car lot, and besides, who would want to buy second-hand American gas-guzzlers with the price of a gallon shooting through the roof, or he could try to start some kind of a desk job from home, writing freelance articles for the local paper as a way of breaking into the newspaper industry, but Susan had long ago told him to forget that idea, he didn't have the gift, there was no way he was going to make a career out of writing, and Basil Kambanis felt wronged, surely he had at least some talent, and Susan stroked his hand tenderly, because, sure, he might be able to write fairly appealing prose, to string some nice sentences together with proper grammar and syntax, "but honey," the topics he chose were almost always totally inappropriate and had nothing to do with the issues of the day in a city plagued by poverty and financial crisis, unemployment and crime— who cared about the ghosts on Petty Island, the buried treasures of eighteenth-century pirates and slave traders?—and his sentences were like railroad tracks, meticulously constructed lines that went on forever, not a period in sight where you could stop to catch your breath, and it's not like he was saying anything incredibly compelling or gripping, anything with teeth, and so one by one his ideas got erased, leaving nothing but smudges on paper, and now here's this check, roosting in his pocket, nestling its petty collection of zeros into the seams, and if he stays in the car any longer he too will become petty, a nobody, the sum total of his life's work a big fat empty hole, a tragic, undeniable zero, zip, zilch—and to escape the weight of those empty rings, he opens the driver's side door and steps out, only to find himself staring smack-dab at a nearly full moon, which for a moment looks like yet another huge, gluttonous, milky white zero hanging over his head, teetering in space like the sword of Damocles.

Basil is lying on his left side in bed facing the window, which tonight feels kind of drafty, he slid the check for twenty-three thousand dollars into his pillowcase and his hand can almost feel the smooth paper through the fabric, and no matter how hard he tries to drop off to sleep his eyes keep springing open, the gears of his mind won't stop cranking, and as Susan turns over in her sleep and rolls onto his side of the bed, he's annoyed yet again by his wife's talent for sleep, how easily and naturally she can always nod off, even in times of crisis, like when Leto had a 104-degree fever that wouldn't come down and they rushed her to the emergency room and she had to stay two nights in the hospital, or when he thought he was having a heart attack, which turned out just to be heartburn, and the doctors gave him some probiotics to help his digestion, or when her father Dave died and they had to get up early and catch the first train to Columbus, and Susan slept like a rock straight through her alarm, and they almost missed the train and the funeral both, and looking at her now with her eyes closed and her hands tucked under her head, crowding in on the few square feet of space in this world where he can rest his body, Basil can suddenly imagine quite easily how she'll be as an old woman, with the arthritis that slender, delicate women often suffer, how her hip might break at seventy-five if she misses a step on the stairs or slips on a freshly mopped floor, can imagine her face crisscrossed by thin, horizontal wrinkles, a head of limp, white, thinning hair, blue eyes that have lost their luster, like a window covered in morning mist, and it occurs to him that what he'd most like to do with the money hidden in his pillow is to buy back some time, a decade or so, to bring back his full, thick, wavy head of hair that's started to go worryingly thin, and as he reaches up to touch the bald spot forming at the back of his head, he turns onto his other side and hugs the pillow tightly to him, and then, since there's no chance of him falling asleep, he gets up to pee and drink some water straight from the tap, because it's a kind of superstition with him, to always replace what he's lost right away.

Basil doesn't flush the toilet for fear of waking the girls, who've started sharing the double bed in Leto's room across the hall, and, walking on tiptoe, he carefully inches his way down the circular staircase, quickens his pace as he crosses the living room, trips over his daughter's schoolbag that she's left lying on the floor, stubs his pinky toe on the corner the sofa, and curses himself for having forgotten to switch on the little blue nightlight before going to bed, and as he enters the kitchen, limping slightly with his right leg, he finds Leto standing with a spoon in her hand in front of the open fridge, pulling down a family-sized jar of peanut butter, and before she can reap the rewards of her midnight raid, Basil plucks the jar from her hands and reminds her of the agreement they made a few years back, after lengthy and heated negotiations, that peanut butter is a necessary evil, a nutritional disgrace that he allows in their home only because it exists in the homes of her classmates and friends, and while Basil would never want to deprive her of anything whose absence would make her feel inferior in any way, that doesn't mean she can shovel in mouthfuls of saturated fats whenever she wants, their agreement was a slice of bread with peanut butter every other day after lunch or dinner, and it's his responsibility to hold her to that, unless she wants the two of them to sit down at the table right now and gorge themselves on the rest of the jar and then never buy another, because peanut butter is for kids, it's a childish taste that Leto needs to let go of, after all, it's been three days since she got her first period and it's time for her to grow up.

So they sit down at the kitchen table with the lights off, the huge jar of peanut butter between them, Leto really only wanted a spoonful, maybe two or three at most, just for the taste, and certainly not half a jar in her stomach, but she forces herself to eat another spoonful, and another, holding back the nausea, taking a deep breath before finally pushing the jar away, that's it, she can't swallow another bite, but Basil keeps going, unphased, as Leto watches, observing his thinning hair, the stray tuft that falls over one eye, and she asks if he's really going to leave them, and Basil keeps the spoon in his mouth for an extra beat to buy time, then answers with riddles and inscrutable words, saying it's not just him, it's her mother, too, sometimes people change, loving couples become enemies, beasts fighting over a meal, but Leto wants to know how they change, and why, and Basil puts his open palm over his mouth as if hesitant to admit that sooner or later dreams die, become practical plans for buying a house or having a baby, getting a station wagon or a summer cottage, and how there's nothing erotic or desirable about a huge, fat, family-sized jar of anything bought on sale at the supermarket, but Leto still isn't satisfied, she wants to know what she can do to convince her mother to get him to stay, and Basil replies that he's seriously considering, actually has made up his mind to move to Greece and open a restaurant there, to build something entirely new, all his own, he deserves a second chance in life, and Leto looks sideways at the jar that's now nearly empty, at Basil's spoon digging awkwardly, insistently at the glass wall of the jar, trying to scrape out a last spoonful—and Leto, who knows her mother well, her coldness and inflexibility, can't imagine her living in that sundrenched land across the Atlantic, and she asks him, begs Basil to take her with him, even just on a trial basis, she doesn't want to be left behind here with her mom, doesn't like her school in East Camden, hates Mrs. Gardner with her dumb exams and ridiculous open-ended questions, she'll enroll in a Greek school, learn Greek, and finally leave behind that idiotic 68 her nutjob mother has been making her carry around all these years, even when other kids make fun of her for it behind her back, and as for soccer, she'll find another, better team to play on, and when she graduates she'll go to university, get a job—"And Minnie?" Basil says, cutting her off, "Are you going to leave your new friend here, all alone?" he asks, playing his final card, and Leto thinks it over for a long time, really thinks about it, and the blood rushes to her cheeks and her eyes fill with tears as she says, "Mom loves her more than me," and then she stands up, crying, accidentally flicking the light on in her confusion, and runs straight to the bathroom to throw up, it's gross, peanut butter is totally gross, and so are her mother and stepfather and all her classmates, everyone around her, no one understands her, no one ever understood her.

And not only is she misunderstood, she can't even call the shots over her own body, her appetites and moods, something awful and overwhelming is happening to her, and the worst thing is that it's out of her control, she hates having to wear a disgusting little diaper called a sanitary pad that's actually not sanitary at all, soaked in the dirty blood her body keeps pushing out regularly and in great quantities, and when Susan told her that this exact thing is going to happen once a month for the rest of her fertile years, which means probably into her fifties, she felt insanely depressed, because how is she supposed to run around on the field with this stupid diaper between her legs that bothers her even when she's just sitting still? For the past three days she's been wishing with all her heart that she were a boy, she already knew that being able to pee standing up was an undeniable advantage, but this new wound is a hit below the belt, and she's now entirely convinced that it's way better to be a boy than a girl, and she wonders why boys would ever be interested in girls to begin with, all she wants is a place where she can go and hide until it's all over, she'll run away from home, leave a short, cryptic note and disappear for a few days, she's so sick of other people deciding things for her, and a sleepy Minnie watches as Leto tosses things into her schoolbag with no rhyme or reason, things that would be totally useless at school, empties the contents of her overstuffed piggy bank into her pocket, then turns and tells Minnie she has an away game today, they're staying over in Philly, and if her parents ask, she won't be home for dinner.

XIV

A vague mist hanging 'round half the pages:
(Sometimes how strange and clear to the soul,
That all these solid things are indeed but apparitions,
concepts, non-realities.)
WALT WHITMAN

The first thought that passed through Antonis Kambanis's mind was that maybe he had some kind of unfinished business with the Italian mafia, but though he wracked his brains trying to figure out what mistake he could still be paying for fifteen years down the road, he kept coming up empty-handed, unable to find a satisfactory answer, much less a logical one, and as the minutes ticked by and the driver crossed the Benjamin Franklin Bridge from Camden into Philadelphia, he became more and more worried, because the mob bosses in that neighboring city of unbrotherly love were cruel and unusual, known for their extreme measures, no less creative or brutal than the stumps of ears or detached fingernails of Manhattan or the sliced-off tongues and missing noses of Brooklyn, and he started to say a silent prayer, though before he could bring his hands together in a posture of penance for his bygone wickedness and sins, the tallest and roughest-looking of the men tied a black handkerchief around his eyes and the car swerved back around, and twenty minutes later it turned onto a bumpy dirt road, and when the man in the passenger seat rolled down his window to ash his cigar Antonis caught a whiff of wet earth, and the car suddenly stopped, but he never got a chance to get out and stretch his legs, since they shoved him into a tiny shed with a few benches and a common toilet, piling him in that shoebox with another ten guys who seemed more or less cut from the same cloth as he, and before long, through a few tentative comments and questions, they discovered they were all bound by a common incriminating element that had probably landed them there in the same mess: every last one of them had Italian papers, and for one reason or another had neglected to apply for American citizenship—and according to the 1918 amendments to the Alien and Sedition Acts of 1798, which restricted the freedoms of foreign-born residents of the new republic, the American government had the right to apprehend, restrain, secure, and remove foreign citizens or residents of either sex over the age of fourteen who had not acquired American citizenship and whose country was currently engaged in armed conflict with the United States.

The truth is usually simple and modest, like mathematical formulas describing the laws of nature, though of course there are causes and effects,

factors both internal and external, known and unknown constants and variables, and whether collective or individual, the truth often keeps company
with untruths that are nonetheless taken by many
to be unshakeable truths, sworn upon as if they
were verifiable facts by those who have learned the
art of wisely combining actual facts with certain
false facts—but Antonis Kambanis, hands crossed
on his chest, didn't have a slick enough tongue or
the chutzpah needed to save his skin, and when his
turn came, he tried in vain to convince the Feds that
his life was a crapshoot, he went where the wind
blew him, he'd ended up in Camden by chance, and
by chance had gotten a job at the New York Shipbuilding Corporation and learned his way around
the warehouses and factory floors of a future wartime industry, twenty years ago he'd been looking
for work and that was the job he found, he'd barely
heard of the Italian mafia or the Irish mob, what was
all this about moonshine and corpses and the illegal
distribution of contraband substances—if he happened to have met a few small-time Italian crooks
here and there, was it his fault if their bosses supported Mussolini, those Italian papers of his are
fake, he's Greek, a diaspora Greek, he was born on
Nisyros, which to his terrible fortune is ruled to
this day by Italy, just like the rest of the Dodecanese,
but he has no truck with Italian or German agents,
and he's never seen a Jap in his life, or if he has, they
probably looked to him like a slant-eyed Chinaman,
he has no idea what they're talking about, what
Irish deafmute, he's Greek, an honest straight
shooter, if he were in Greece right now he'd be

fighting on the side of the Allies, and he didn't en-
list here because no one ever asked him to, it just
didn't happen, who in his right mind wants to fight
phantom enemies at the risk of his own life, all he
wants is a roof over his head like everyone else, a bit
of cash, a steady job, a quiet life, and to see his son
achieve a bit more than he has, though he can't complain, he's done well for himself, he's a law-abiding
entrepreneur with three shops to his name, or two
and a half, let's say two, of course he pays his taxes,
and he's been married for seven years to a Greek
woman from Mytilini, here's the wedding ring, it's
solid silver, why don't they believe him, damn it all,
what business does he have being shipped off to a
relocation camp for alien enemies in Montana or
Tennessee, he's no traitor or agent or saboteur, and
if he never got his citizenship papers in order it was
simply because he forgot, he just didn't get around
to it, it never crossed his mind that it was necessary
or obligatory, definitely more American than Greek,
he'll do it now, he'll fill out the application and pay
the fee—"Now," he says, and he means it, but as he
raises his voice to underline the injustice being
committed, the door shuts and a hand lifts him up
and lands him with a kick in the pants back on the
bench to wait.

To his great luck he wasn't sent to Montana, where
they were mostly imprisoning German Americans,
while camps for Japanese Americans had opened in
California, Idaho, Wyoming, and Arkansas, and
though by June, 1942, one thousand five hundred
and twenty Italians had also been relocated, Antonis
Kambanis was not among them, having had at least

a bit of fortune in his misfortune: while he was waiting for the Feds to pronounce their verdict, he was recognized by an old Italian mafia guy who was now an FBI informer, Mussolini had gotten a bee in his bonnet about the mafia and they about him, and the mob bosses, with the jailed Lucky Luciano as their ringleader or kingpin, had convinced President Roosevelt that they should all work together to fight the Nazis, commies, and fascists for the good of democracy, and that's just what ended up happening, the US government was already building bridges with Sicilian mafia families, preparing the ground for the Allied invasion of Sicily, Hitler's soft underbelly, with General Eisenhower at the helm of the crafty and cunning Operation Mincemeat, and as for the commies in France, they all had a bright-red target on their backs, they wouldn't dare try to lay a hand on the old port or the suspicious shipments of Paul Carbone or Salvatore Greco, because their brothers-in-arms from the Corsican mafia in Marseilles would eat them alive. At any rate, way back in 1919, this mafia guy who was now an informer with strong connections to the mob bosses Luciano and Carbone had offered Antonis a job and a place to sleep if he would do a few odd jobs for him in Hell's Kitchen, and he'd always prided himself on his ability to remember a face even if he'd only seen it once, he had a photographic memory, no detail ever escaped him, so he recognized Antonis right away and decided to corroborate his story and put in a good word with the Feds, because this poor Greek seemed just as downtrodden and miserable as he'd been all those years before.

And so after three days that felt more like a week, they loaded Antonis onto a rickety bus and sent him back to Camden, and he walked an hour and a half from where they dropped him off back to his house, it was the crack of dawn and there were no municipal buses at that hour, and when he hobbled up to the house and let himself in he didn't say a word, just shut himself in the bathroom, washed, dressed, combed his hair, and went back out two hours later to give his information and fingerprints at the nearest post office, as if he were some known criminal who had committed heinous crimes, and they confiscated his old identity card, took his photograph so they'd have a recent one on file, and issued him a new identification certificate that he was required to carry on his person at all times, rain or shine, and which declared him to be an enemy alien, one of the roughly 1,100,000 foreigners listed in the US Department of Justice's enemy alien registry, who were either shipped off to internment camps or allowed to circulate with certain restrictions, and from now on their entire lives and livelihoods would depend on their current and future meekness and modesty with regard to the American nation.

But during those three days that seemed like a week, something inside of him broke that could never again be repaired, as if he'd simply given up on the things of this world. He never again raised a hand against Rallou, and he stopped going to the coffee house, he might pass by every now and then to say hello, but without much interest, and he followed the news but without the same fervency, as if none of it had much to do with him any longer. He wasn't depressed, he had just reached the limits of his endurance, had no energy left for sympathy or outrage, anger or worry, things at the shop were going well enough, and he held on to it for the small salary and end-of-year bonus when profits allowed, but he didn't bring the same zest and zeal to his work, and over time he began to hunch and shrink a smidge, lost three or four pounds, which slowly became six or eight, he just didn't have his old appetite, especially now that every waking hour seemed to be spent on financial headaches, his partner Takis was starting to lose his marbles, all signs pointed in the direction of rapidly advancing Alzheimer's, and meanwhile Rallou kept trying to get her drinking under control, but every time she cut back her demons returned even stronger than before, haunting her until she went out into the street and doused passersby with bitter comments and vulgar curses, and Basil, who in the spring of 1943 had just turned five, would hide her bottles in cupboards and drawers, under mattresses and beneath beds, behind doors and on windowsills, but Rallou had the nose of a mole, could close her eyes and sniff out the booze in an instant, she had a sixth sense for the stuff that even the FBI couldn't beat.

While the Allies were fighting to break through the Winter Line in Italy and capture Rome, Antonis Kambanis sold his share of the store in Liberty Park so as to be able to nurse Takis through his final days and cover the funeral expenses, he owed it to him, and as he cleaned out the home of his friend and long-time partner, he found an old, well-preserved Victrola and a handful of dusty records with hand-written labels reading *Enrico,* and he brought them home, and a few hours after the funeral, with a young, anxious Basil tying and untying his laces and Rallou lying silent on the sofa all in black, he decided to break the silence, to banish the frigid winter that had sunk into the walls and furniture, and Enrico Caruso's warm voice leapt out of the gramophone, wrapping them in its bewitching balm—they had no idea that in 1830s Paris the winter was likewise mercilessly cold and claimed the love and life of a pallid, consumptive seamstress named Mimì, and as the needle scratched its steady path over the record, a discordant note cracked through the melody, the singing stopped, and a different voice called out, "From the top, Enrico," and *La Bohème* fell silent, marked by this moment of failure, and no matter how many records he tried on the gramophone he always encountered some flaw, some shortfalling, because all the records were defective takes that had ended up in the trash, recording sessions that had been aborted because something went wrong, a false start, a rushed note, a catch in the throat, a missed cue, and Antonis Kambanis insisted on trying record after record, he simply couldn't understand why his partner had kept this collection of someone else's mistakes, until at some point Rallou couldn't bear it any longer, her temper snapped and she shouted, "I can't take any more of this," and little Basil clapped his hands over his ears, ran to his father, fell to the ground on his knees, and begged him to make the voices stop.

And the voices did stop, and spring came, April brought a new calm, and when people started knocking on doors all over Dudley, Marlton, and Parkside, collecting old pots and pans and scraps of metal to support the battles still raging in Europe, Africa, and Asia, Rallou handed over her dowry, two frying pans and her one big pot, leaving their home without the items necessary for her to cook their daily meals, and when Antonis Kambanis found out he didn't say a word, didn't react, just went out and bought a new pot and pan to replace them; May was a sweet, lovely month, news from the front was encouraging, and every two weeks Kambanis presented himself to the authorities and stood in line to put another signature under the phrase *Enemy Alien*, then made his way back to the shop in Dudley, and at midday walked over to Parkside to see how things were getting on there; June came on strong, the weather grew warmer, he would often leave his jacket hanging on the back of his chair in the morning, and one evening when a light rain began falling while he was walking home he nearly caught a cold, but he was a tough nut, his immune system was strong and shook off the germs; then on June 4, 1944, the United States 5th Army liberated Rome, and the same afternoon Rallou badly burned both her right hand and the green beans she'd forgotten on the stove, and to top it all off the next morning Basil fell ill with a 102-degree fever—and despite a whole host of minor warnings barely worth mentioning, nothing truly foretold what would follow when on June 6, with Basil still ill and Antonis Kambanis drowning in work for a charity ball to support the wives of injured sailors, and as American, British, and Canadian forces were attempting a coordinated landing at Normandy under the command of General Eisenhower, Rallou made the best stuffed vegetables of her life, turned the radio on low to listen to Telly Savalas on *Your Voice of America*, fixed herself a plate of food, poured a glass of red wine that her gracious and compassionate cousin had sent to her on the sly, sat down by the window, and ate the pepper first and then the tomato, as her mother always had, leaving the two small, crunchy potatoes for last, with a bit of soft, salty feta, and she drank all the wine, a liter in one sitting, and through her drunken haze and confusion she felt like she was no longer in the United States, because there was Greek coming across on the radio, and the tomatoes were sweet and juicy and the peppers as fresh and fragrant as if she had just picked them from her uncle's garden, the potatoes had soaked up the oil and softened under their crust, and someone was passing by the window who looked like her older brother, the spitting image of Andreas right there in broad daylight in Dudley, dear Lord, when had he arrived, how long had he been looking for her—and she rose to her feet with her apron still on, and, staggering, opened the door and ran out into the yard to greet him.

XV

lone red-winged blackbird
riding a reed in high tide—
billowing clouds
NICK VIRGILIO

Chaos reigns at the home of Susan Miller and Basil
Kambanis, it's after nine and there's still no sign of
Leto, and the one-sentence note smudged with
peanut butter that she left on the kitchen counter—*I'm out of here*—together with Minnie's message
about Leto's team going on an overnight trip to
Philadelphia sent Susan and Basil into a tailspin,
Susan called the school, where no one knew anything about a game, Basil called the coach and
learned that, yes, there'd been talk of meeting a team
in Philly for a scrimmage last month, but the trip
had been called off for lack of funds, does he have
any idea how much a hotel room costs over there,
twice, even three times as much as in Camden, they
might as well go to Boston or Washington, and Basil
cradles the receiver, Susan is at a loss, and the two of

them look suspiciously at Minnie, perhaps secretly blaming her arrival for the mess they're in as a family, but they don't dare say it out loud, Susan is pacing back and forth in the kitchen and Basil opens the back door just in case they've made some mistake and Leto is actually right where she should be, out there in the yard kicking a ball against the fence, and Minnie feels like she's intruding but has nowhere else to go, her hands curl into fists, she's clenching her teeth, sitting on the very edge of the couch, trying to take up as little space as she can, to become invisible, if only she could wander unseen through the streets, duck into houses and swipe uneaten food off the plates of the families inside, sleep in a ball on the corners of king-sized beds, maybe borrow an outfit every so often, and when she grew taller and the old ones no longer fit, she would make sure to bring them all back, and it would just be until she grew up and didn't need anyone anymore, Susan calls the police to report the disappearance but it hasn't been twenty-four hours yet, they need to wait at least another three or four before they can go down to the station, Basil suggests that they get in the car and drive over to Philly—and this whole time, during all this panic and confusion, Leto has been trying to get comfortable in the big metal storage cabinet with the garden tools and the old, slightly moldy mattress they've got rolled up in there just in case—she's managed to wrap herself up so that only the unruly ends of her blond hair are peeking out, and only her breath is audible, hissing and uneven, her throat scratchy from the dust and mites in the cabinet and the ancient mattress, she should've brought her inhaler, goddammit, it would feel so good to take a nice sharp inhale to calm things down, but she'll manage, she can stay hidden, she'll keep it up for as long as she can.

Her body has gone numb, it's not easy to sit still and silent in the same sad spot, so she stands, stretches her arms, shakes her legs, it's been two hours and she's yawning with boredom and discomfort, then she slips back into her black spiral hole, her little burrow at the heart of this moth-eaten mattress, leans her head back and prays for her parents to die, a fateful curve in the road, a moment of poor judgement on the wet pavement, then she takes a deep breath and changes her mind, no, she doesn't want them to die, she wants to save them from a certain death that only she can foresee, pull them out of the burning car and give them mouth-to-mouth right there on the spot, putting her own life in danger because the car is about to explode, but that's still not enough, and she sinks a bit deeper into the mattress, she'll die, that's it, she'll die a sudden, unexpected death and her funeral will be their punishment on earth, and once she's dead she'll find it in her heart to forgive them for all the bitterness and disappointment they caused, she'll stand off to the side and cry with them, because of course she'll be there, too, watching the service, accepting people's condolences even though she hates funerals, at the one funeral she happened to attend, the funeral of her grandfather from Columbus, her cousins looked at her as if she were from outer space and asked her the stupidest questions, what did the name Leto mean and what kind of dorky, retarded name was it anyhow, and her dead grandfather's brother gave her a sloppy kiss on the cheek and pinched her behind, and her Aunt Mary scolded her for wearing sneakers and sitting with her legs open, which apparently wasn't ladylike—and as she remembers it all the blood rushes to her head, she hates every one of them, though she also wonders if anyone will miss her, certainly not her teammates, and what's the use in staying in here any longer, her stomach is grumbling, her hunger is giving her a headache, and it's dark and depressing being cooped up in this stupid closet, she can't even take a proper breath, but then again coming back out won't accomplish anything either, she needs to teach them a lesson, and so she sinks even further in, closes her eyes, and falls asleep.

Minnie has never been to Philadelphia, it's unfamiliar territory she's seen only in newspapers and magazines, and as Basil's old station wagon turns onto Washington Lane headed east and drives past the track at Roosevelt Middle School, it seems to Minnie that Philly isn't all that different from Camden, though maybe the proportions are a bit off, there are more buildings, and they're taller, the streets are wider and cleaner, and as she sucks in information through the car window, she searches to find someone who might be her father, looking for herself in every middle-aged black man they pass, she's glued her palms to the glass and stares out at the streets and buildings, not wanting to waste this sole chance she's been given as Basil drives slowly and carefully through the streets, Roosevelt Middle School is closed, the lights are off, the rent-a-cop at the door studies Leto's photograph and shakes his head, Susan has rolled her window down and is leaning halfway out the window, and keeps telling Basil to slow down, slow down, but how slow can he go, a silent tension electrifies the car as three disconnected shapes hang from three different windows, it's nearly dawn and the car is running on fumes, Basil Kambanis pulls into a twenty-four-hour Exxon station to fill the tank and charge it to his card, and while Susan goes in to use the bathroom Minnie watches a homeless man who could be her father, she thinks he looks like her but isn't sure, she's about to open the door and ask his name and if he remembers her, but she's afraid, and besides, she's not even sure they really do look alike, actually she's not at all sure now that she's had a better look, there are fine abrasions on his face, a crust of dried blood on his chin, he's wearing a torn, dirty winter coat, and before she can decide what to do, Susan opens the door and gets in and Basil starts the engine, they're headed back to Camden where they'll drive straight to the police station.

Pete squirms in the hallway of the precinct in Marlton, they've cuffed him behind his back, but that's not what's bothering him, or even his crooked jaw or broken ribs from the officer's billy club and kicks, what's really gotten under his skin, what's driving him nuts, what he wants to know more than anything is what asshole ratted him out, it's not like they just caught him with a stolen car or something, even a nice one, tonight they met in Gateway to dole out the goods, the crack and the dope he was supposed to push, a hundred grams at fifteen percent, it was his last trial as a dealer on the streets, and then he'd get to form his own crew, he'd be a prince, and within five years he'd have moved another step up, to king, a full-blown Quiñón with his own posse for protection, he just needed things to go well tonight and everything else would follow, girls, money, cars, he'd be living it up like Fatso, Don Juan, and the Mayor, who just sit around busting his balls, sending him out on these stupid errands, they know he has the best connections in the schools to sell weed, so why are they giving him heroin, who's he supposed to push that on, you'd have to be a real loser to be shooting up at twelve or thirteen—sure, there's some movement for crack, something happening in the yard during recess, and now he's like a beast in a cage, howling, growling, down on the ground, how the fuck did he end up here, "fuck it all, you assholes, just fuck," they nailed him and took his share of the load and any dough he had on him too, he screwed it all up, right when he was coming into his own, and out of the whole crew he's the only one who got caught, the fuzz didn't nab anyone else, it must have been an inside job, for sure, clear as day, those fags, there's no way he's avoiding the slammer, but he'd fuck them all over, they'd have him to deal with, at most he'd end up in juvie outside of Camden, who gave a shit, worst case he'd be in for a few years, and when he got out he'd fuck them all up—and while the cop who picked him up and gave him that first, stinging blow on the jaw with his club nudges him with his foot to stand up and shoves him into a blindingly white, six-by-six interrogation office, Basil and Susan are down the hall reporting the disappearance of their daughter Leto Kambanis, a minor, and Minnie is filing a statement, telling them whatever she knows and imagines as the last person to have seen her, and the officer on duty for the morning shift asks if she noticed anything out of the ordinary during the past week, if Leto had said or done anything out of the ordinary, or if she'd seen anything strange in the neighborhood, and Minnie nods, "Yes, of course," old lady Melrose next door still has her Christmas lights up in the living room, and she talks to her cats as if they're her sons John and Michael who vanished into the rice paddies of Vietnam, and Leto sold her collection of baseball cards to get money for her trip to Greece, and as Minnie talks, she crosses and uncrosses her legs, and finally asks if it's okay for her to go to the bathroom, it's an emergency, and the officer points to the door and says, "Down the hall, turn right, last door on the left," but Minnie gets confused and turns the wrong way, then opens the first door on the left where there's a key hanging in the lock and finds herself staring straight into the face of her brother Pete, whose hands are cuffed behind his back, and his jaw is crooked and smashed, and all she manages to say through her surprise and fear is a choked, muffled, "Pete—Mom—," and she opens her arms to hug him, she's missed him, she misses them all, her mother, the father she never met, and her brother Pete, too, but he, like a bull seeing red, rushes at her and slams her with all his weight into the metal door, and Minnie stumbles and falls to her knees, he's kicking her wildly in the ribs, all over her body, and Minnie shrinks and rolls up into a tight ball like a spineless little grub, sliding out of range, leaving behind a hot yellow stream as she drags herself off and rises to her feet and, trembling, stumbles away, leaving the door hanging ajar behind her, and she would like, oh how she would like to have shut it all the way.

XVI

(Say, O mother! have I not to your thought been faithful?
Have I not, through life, kept that alone before me?)
—WALT WHITMAN

She's trapped in a bed in West Jersey Hospital, where
head nurse Mrs. Hocevar and the floor nurse on duty
are changing her dressings and bandages, tending
to surface wounds that will all have healed in a week
or two, her condition is stable, and while Rallou
Kambanis has regained her senses she shows no
inclination to speak, the surgeon assigned to her
case blames it on the shock of her accident, says it's
just a matter of time before her speech returns—
though she'll never again be able to move her limbs,
the blow to the nape of her neck did irreparable
damage, the paralysis is complete and irreversible,
and they still haven't shared that news with her,
there's simply no point given the state she's in. Yet
two days ago when she was rushed to the hospital
and her husband appeared hours later—a poor fool
caught at sea during a storm, hanging onto his

old-fashioned three-piece suit and his mediocre, thickly accented English as if they were life jackets—the doctor took him aside and explained there was no hope his wife would ever walk again, they would have to arrange their lives according to these new circumstances, and he asked the head nurse to explain to Mr. Kambanis precisely what he meant by this, and Mrs. Hocevar looked the patient's husband straight in the eye, this Antonis who was once a Nondas, and saw the fear there, the panic and desperation, and she forgave him everything, took him by the arm, and pulled him gently into the long and uninviting corridor, where they walked up and down and she explained what his life would be like from now on, and Antonis Kambanis, his hat in his hand, fiddling nervously with the brim, stopped her midway, raising his eyes and searching desperately for something to grab hold of, some hidden clue, some fluttering eyelid that would cast doubt on what she was saying so he could build a counterargument in his mind, could find the courage to tell her that miracles do happen, no matter what science says, that things could change from one minute to the next, that life could flip things upside down again on a dime, that there's always room for hope.

There was in fact no room for hope, as soon became clear: Rallou could move only her eyes and mouth, her words were now her only strength, though her wants had hands that kept seeking, and her thoughts had feet that constantly pursued, and whenever she was in one of her fits of depression, she would fall silent and wait for the alcohol to come, and since they had reduced her daily ration, though they didn't cut it out entirely, she could go whole hours without saying a word, and only when she screamed and howled frightening, inarticulate howls, insisting her arms and legs were in terrible pain, would Antonis Kambanis give her a few sips, he'd given little Basil orders to tip tiny shot glasses of ouzo or wine into her mouth, whatever they had on hand, and he always made sure there was something to drink in the cupboard, it was his wife's sedative, her salve, and Rallou would go as calm as a baby in a cradle, but when she emerged again from the sweet drowsiness of drink she would begin a slow, otherworldly dirge, a mourning song, and would wail the hours away until evening when her husband came home, and then she would beg him, screaming, to kill her, to set her free from this daily, unbearable misery, and Basil would pray for her to die in her sleep, and when he turned six and went to school for the very first time, he finally felt a weight lifting from his body, a dark shadow slipping away, but the other kids quickly found out about his situation at home, and from one day to the next he became a laughingstock, an outcast, the butt of endless jokes, subject to constant cruelty for being the son of a drunk, retarded mother, and soon enough the misery of his home life followed him everywhere, he carried a cross at home and climbed a Golgotha all day at school, and that's when he became a devout little Christian, it helped him put up with the teasing and the cruelty, the curses and the threats, let him hold on to the hope that one day he'd be transformed into a superhero and everyone would discover his vengeful powers, and so he endured his paralyzed mother's curses and shouts, her demands that he bring her the bedpan or comb her hair, or wash and clean her, and since his father was barely ever home anymore, bit by bit Basil had to learn the rest of the household chores, a home needed to be clean and tidy, and there needed to be a home-cooked meal on the table each night, because all their strength as a family, their Greekness, their dignity itself lay piled there in that plate of hot, nourishing, time-honored, traditional food.

Now that a victory for the Allied Forces seemed to be assured, just a matter of months if not weeks away, and since the doctor insisted that he talk to his wife about cheerful, familiar things, when Antonis Kambanis returned home from work in the evenings he would read his wife bits of the Greek-language *National Herald* or the newsletter of the local Greek community, turning straight to the society page full of weddings, baptisms, and grand openings of new stores, and when they finished with these celebrations, he would switch to the Allied successes and any political news out of Greece, anything that seemed to bear even an indirect relation to them, like a piece about the signing of the Caserta Agreement on September 26, 1944, between the exiled Greek government and the military leaders of resistance organizations EAM and EDES, an agreement overseen by the British Armed Forces in the Mediterranean in light of the upcoming Axis defeat and liberation of Greece from German occupation, an agreement that put all resistance forces under the control of the Government of National

Unity, which would in turn need to obey the orders of General Ronald Scobie, leader of the British liberation forces in Greece—and as Antonis lowers the newspaper and lets it fall to his knees, because he's sick and tired of all these names and acronyms and details falling down on him like a pitiless rain, Rallou asks him to come over, lift her up, and set her down in her wheelchair, but Antonis hesitates, it's late, after two in the morning, the boy is sleeping in his room, but his wife insists, she wants to go outside and get some fresh air, and while Kambanis stands there silent and still, Rallou tries in vain to lift her hips, to gather some force, to turn over, to roll her body like a barrel to the edge of the sofa, and Kambanis stands up slowly, as if he has all the time in the world, bends down over her, then kneels, embraces her carefully, lifts her slight, fragile weight into the wheelchair, and opens the door. There's an upright sliver of a moon in the sky, the wheels roll over the asphalt and the couple moves like a pair of acrobats balancing on the white dividing line in the middle of the road, they're like opposing armies that need one another to exist, and as they circle the block in the silent, unstirring night, Rallou asks him out of the blue whether he would ever trust a person named Scobie, what kind of name is that, anyhow, where does it come from, and her interest is surprising but genuine, and Antonis doesn't respond, because he has nothing to say, it's never crossed his mind what the name Scobie might mean, and at the end of the day he doesn't care— though in fact nothing good can come from a name that means *prickly*, with roots in a village that's long since disappeared, wiped off the map, in a Scottish land now lost to time.

And so, every now and then, late on nights when it wasn't raining or snowing and the temperature didn't dip below freezing, they would put their son to bed and then take the wheelchair out for a walk around the block, and when the weather was nice Antonis would put lawn chairs outside on the weekends for them to sunbathe side by side, and once, on a gentle night in October, during a stretch of Indian summer when Kambanis was in good spirits, they got as far as the river, stared across for a long while at the crystalline shore of Philadelphia, then silently headed back. He loved her for her sadness, and his pity, guilt, and the passing years had softened him, and on Rallou's prematurely aged and wrinkled face—she was, after all, several years older than him—he could see the sadness and despair of his own middle-aged mother whom he had left behind twenty-five years ago, in hunger and poverty, dependent on the kindness of strangers and the mercy of relatives, and the more he mulled over the past, the more he swore to stay by Rallou's side to the end, pushing the wheelchair every few days over sidewalks and streets, uphill and down, and on Sundays, in the early afternoon, just before the streets filled with the joyous shouts of young families, he would take his own family—son, wife, and wheelchair—and they would walk down to the Omonia Patisserie to get a soft drink, or a bowl of ice cream, or some other treat.

It was the beginning of November, 1944, Roosevelt had just won his fourth term in the White

House with Harry Truman as Vice President, Basil Kambanis had just gotten his first three stitches after a big annoying bully of a classmate threw a rock at him, and Antonis Kambanis hired an Armenian to manage the Parkside store, it was too much for him to take care of both locations on his own, he needed help with the ordering and errands, and Arsen was easygoing, trustworthy, and polite, not one to complain or to squander his modest wages at coffee houses and taverns, he was saving up to open a place of his own, and he'd surely do well, he had a knack for business, and so Antonis Kambanis had more time on his hands, and wanted more than anything to teach his son the tricks of the trade, to inspire him with the entrepreneurial spirit, he saw how Basil struggled day and night with his studies, and while his son claimed to have a talent for writing, drawing, and art in general, Antonis wasn't so sure, book learning didn't seem to be Basil's forte, and Kambanis had no great opinion of his teacher, a young Irish lass who puffed up the boy's head with made-up stories, some happy and some sad, about wild men, pirates, penniless downtrodden revolutionaries, and besides, Basil was left-handed, a bad omen at a moment when the Russians were imposing their imperialist claims on the West, with local infiltrators inflaming hearts and minds in the unions and clubs—according to Arsen the Feds kept secret lists with the names of strikers and instigators, and Antonis Kambanis, who was terrified of lists and files, acted right away on this information: he forced Basil to start holding his pencil with his right hand, and whenever the boy forgot or crossed himself with his left hand, Antonis would smack his wrist with a wooden spoon that was always lying on the table for precisely that purpose, and when he realized that even the *National Herald* had started drifting leftwards, he cancelled his monthly subscription, and from then on bought only the hardline *Atlantis*, which exalted the manly exploits of liberated Greece, glorified the Allied liberators and British guarantors, and sought the return of King George II to the throne—and all this simply because Antonis Kambanis wanted no more dealings with the Feds, wanted to keep himself on the side of order, in good standing with those in power, in the US and in his homeland, too.

When the war finally ended and the Germans hastened to sign an unconditional surrender at Potsdam, and it was a matter of time and practical arrangements until the Dodecanese, including his island of Nisyros, became part of Greece, Antonis Kambanis got swept up in the celebratory atmosphere of general jubilation and excitement, and he promised his son that, God willing, they would soon set off on a transatlantic journey, and he really hoped they would manage it, even just once, he wanted his son to see the land where he himself had been born and raised, and he also nursed a secret hope to visit the grave of his mother Foteinoula, sometimes he could hear her in his sleep, tossing and turning, gasping and wheezing about the dried-up oil and long-extinguished flame of the lamp on her grave.

That trip to Nisyros never happened, the boat trip to Greece alone would have taken over a week and

the money for the fare could cover their expenses in
Camden for nearly two months, and it wasn't that
Antonis Kambanis was stingy, but business had
fallen off as the economy got back on its feet, people
wanted new shoes and clothes, their old things were
reminders of a period of hardship, struggle, and
deprivation that they'd prefer to put behind them,
and then there were those damned machines that
could stitch things up in no time at all and at half
the price, and Antonis, who always counted his
earnings by hand, saw less and less in the cash box
each time, according to his calculations his
monthly profits had fallen by as much as twenty-five
percent, but he had promised his only son a trip and
he couldn't bear to go back on his word, so in July of
1946 they rented an automatic sedan and drove
down to Tampa, Florida, got a room at a motel two
miles from the beach, went swimming and sun-
bathed and explored the town, and during that
week when Arsen took care of both stores and
stayed nights with Rallou at the house, their daily
routines and habits took on the rosy color of a craw-
fish or lobster, until it came time to return and the
only conversations they'd had all that time were
about what to eat and where to go, if the water was
warm, the chairs comfortable, the mattress firm,
and when they tossed their suitcases and dirty
clothes into the trunk and got back into the sedan
for the trip home, Antonis Kambanis gripped the
wheel tightly in his hands and sealed his mouth
into a pinched, silent line, the sunburn on his
shoulders and peeling arms and back were bothering him, like marks of guilt and shame, traces of

inhibitions and compromises, and when they had passed Washington and were just three hours from home, he stopped the car on the side of the road, took off his short-sleeved shirt, pulled a wrinkled and stained long-sleeved button-up out of the bag of dirty laundry and put it on, and when they arrived in Camden and pulled up in front of the Thrifty car rental, he had his son come and sit beside him in the passenger seat, made him kiss a cross and promise his beloved Christ, put his hand on his heart and swear that no matter what happened, no matter what obstacles he might find in his path, one day he would return to Greece and find his grandmother's grave, and he would do it above all for his father, Antonis Kambanis, son of Vassilis, who always intended to make that journey home but just couldn't do it, never found the courage to return.

XVII

removing
the bullet-proof vest:
the heat
NICK VIRGILIO

Leto is tired of hiding in the storage chest, she's
bored stiff, and her body is stiff too, her legs heavy
and unbending, like pliers, so she climbs up and out
of the mattress, pushes the metal door open, and
finally breathes in a lungful of clean, fresh air—
what joy!—makes herself breakfast and scarfs it
down in the kitchen, thumbing through yesterday's
sports pages, pulls on a sweatsuit, gets her backpack ready, then sits and waits quietly and patiently
for her parents to return, it's already seven, and if
they take any longer she'll miss her first class, not
that she really cares, but something tells her, she's
pretty sure that at least for a while she needs to play
along, play the adults' game—and at that very
moment she hears a key in the door, and it opens,
and Susan and Basil and Minnie come into the

house and see Leto with her backpack slung over her shoulder, tying her laces, and for an instant, just a moment, somewhere between six and ten seconds, no one says anything, and then Susan rushes at her in a fury and pounds her furiously on the back, on the face and head, and Basil springs forward to grab Susan, pulls her back, and slaps her, and Leto doesn't defend herself, doesn't even move, just keeps tying her laces, or rather unties them and ties them again, because she'd made the bow too loose and uneven and she wants a strong, tight knot, perfectly symmetrical, but her hands are trembling and her fingers keep sliding around like they've given up on her altogether, and Minnie, who knows a fair bit about knots, especially the Gordian kind, comes over, kneels down beside Leto, and ties a pair of tight, strong double-knots on her shoes, so they won't come untied and she won't trip and fall, and Leto, who always has trouble saying thank you, the words get stuck in her throat, breaks down and the knot dissolves into a flood of messy tears, halting *thank you*s and muffled *I'm sorry*s.

Basil Kambanis and Susan Miller are talking heatedly under the old mulberry tree, Basil pacing back and forth in its shade, opening and closing his mouth, gesturing wildly with his hands and arms, but nothing he's saying is really of interest to Susan, who watches him coldly, unmoved, hands crossed on her chest, until suddenly she goes on the attack, what's he going to do in Greece, he's crazy, his life is here, and her life and her daughter's life too, there's no way she's going to let him take Leto with him, he can forget about that, just wipe it out of his mind, who cares what Leto wants or what she told him, she's only thirteen, and besides, his parents are the ones who came to the US for a better life, what is he trying to prove, he has no right trying to tell her what to do or how to raise her child, Leto is *her* child, yes, hers, and what has he ever done with his life, nothing, except to turn *her* child into his own spitting image, stubborn and self-centered, and she's perfectly willing to play bad cop again, and he can be goddamn sure that a day will come when Leto will thank her for it, and Basil stands there, head bent, hands shoved deep in his pockets, looking sideways at the big kitchen window where Leto is standing and watching them like a judge, backpack still hanging from one shoulder, and for a moment he shakes his head in regret, then steps toward Susan and touches her shoulder, why don't they call a truce for a few weeks while they sell the house, pack things up, deal with the practical side of things, the money, the divorce, and who knows, maybe they'll change their minds, maybe things will get better, it's when times get tough that couples find out how tightly they're bound to one another, how strong families can be, but instead of smiling, Susan doubles down, gives him a friendly, almost condescending pat on the back, no, she's thought it over, she and Leto are going to move to Vermont, they'll rent a small apartment in Jericho, an old friend found her a decent job at the Bentley Snowflake Museum, there's a good, affordable school for Leto to go to, maybe even as a boarding student, and bit by bit they'll build their life again, without him—"Do you understand?"—on their own.

Basil hunches as he walks through the big super-market in Cramer Hill, Susan hates doing the weekly shopping so it's his job to keep the fridge stocked and the cupboards full, and Leto, who sometimes comes with him, has a sore throat and a slight fever, so Susan, who doesn't want her daughter to rack up any more absences at school, has forbidden her from leaving the house, and so Minnie came with him instead, Susan needed some time and space away from everyone and everything, and while he'd truthfully like some time to himself, too, as soon as Susan suggested the girl ride along she said yes and got ready in a flash, Minnie loves going food shopping, she and Louisa used to put together long lists that they always forgot at home, and then they'd stroll through the aisles for ages, comparing prices, filling their cart with family-sized packs that were cheaper and lasted longer, and Minnie tags behind Basil, scanning the shelves, the new, colorful items, and it strikes her how different, how much cleaner and larger the Cramer Hill supermarket is than the Mamacita in Centerville where they used to shop, which was small, dark, and dirty, owned by a middle-aged, potbellied Puerto Rican and his loud-mouthed wife, and the selection wasn't as good, and while Minnie is absorbed in these comparisons, reaching out every so often to touch a shelf or package, Basil walks ahead, lost as always in his thoughts, and then absentmindedly turns a corner and disappears, vanishes from her field of vision, and in an instant Minnie is all alone in the world, and she's gripped by panic, flooded with insecurity, her heart starts to beat faster, as if it were trying to flap its wings and fly away, all she has in her pocket is a single dime, left over from the last allowance her mother ever gave her, and she's kept the coin as a charm in the pocket of her winter coat to touch whenever she feels sad, and she begins to walk faster, passing shelf after shelf, moving through aisle after aisle looking for Basil, but all she sees is a man too tall to be him, and then another with a white beard, and a well-dressed woman, and she pushes them aside and keeps going, now she's running breathlessly from aisle to aisle, Basil is somewhere up ahead of her, three or four aisles to the right, sunk in his shadowy, dead-end thoughts, and Minnie sees him from a distance, recognizes his heavy form and dark coat, slightly worn and faded at the elbows and collar, and she exhales, runs and grabs his sleeve and all of a sudden feels so much concentrated joy that she begins to quietly cry.

Susan pulls a wool blanket over Leto, who is still feverish, sits beside her and takes her hand, and explains to her gently that Greece is far away, and not a welcoming place, it wouldn't suit them, it would be a shame to throw their future away out of the stubbornness and optimism of youth, does Leto have any idea how often Susan has regretted abandoning her studies, never getting her degree, she thought she had her whole life in front of her, she couldn't possibly be making a mistake, she followed her gut, only her gut was wrong, it always sent her running after men and ideas, and this time she's not going to make the same mistake, she's going to stay here and fight, and it might be hard at first, but things will get easier, "Are we going to leave Camden?" Leto asks, and Susan nods, "Where are we going?" Leto wants to know, "Vermont," Susan answers, "Okay, but I'm leaving that 68 behind, no more dumb middle name," Leto says, and Susan nods again, "Promise?" Leto insists, and Susan promises, "I'm sorry, I know, it was a mistake," and then there's a long pause, a minor rearrangement of forces, a calculation of what's going and what's staying behind, and Leto looks at the dirt caked under her nails and asks one final question, "Is Minnie coming with us to Vermont?" without really knowing whether or not she wants her new friend to come along, she does but also she doesn't, and the doesn't is probably stronger, no, she definitely doesn't, and Susan takes both of her daughter's hands in her own and tells Leto what the girl wants deep down to hear, "No, Minnie will stay here, she'll find another family."

Basil hadn't intended to make a stop on their way home with half the groceries in the trunk needing the fridge or freezer, but the radio is on and the announcer just reminded him that it's the first of March, he'd entirely forgotten, and then Nicka-phonic Nick read a short little poem on air called a haiku which has a strange form and fixed rules, and Basil knows nothing about poetry, it was never his strong suit, he's a fan of cheap paperbacks, but that poem sticks in his head, and as he turns the corner of Mickle Boulevard and South 3rd Street and brakes at the stop sign in front of the final home of Walt Whitman, which has recently been restored and opened as a museum, he scans the street and inwardly repeats those three metrical lines, *"the blind musician / extending an old tin cup / collects a snowflake,"* then turns on the heat and switches off the radio, because they're passing through a tunnel on the expressway and there's static on the air and ice on the streets, and they take the exit for Fairview, overlooking Newton Creek and Morgan Village and the dead husks of boats of all sizes that at some point ran aground, were pulled up onto shore and left to rust in the ship graveyard, and Basil turns onto a dark side street and parks the car in front of the poorly maintained Hope Nursing Home, and Minnie hesitates, but Basil gestures for her not to be afraid, to unbuckle her seat belt and get out of the car, and Minnie does, because she can trust him, and together they walk up and say hello to the guard on duty, then step almost in unison into a gray and dimly lit building called Hope.

XVIII

Great is Life, real and mystical, wherever and whoever;
Great is Death—sure as life holds all parts together,
Death holds all parts together.
Has Life much purport?—Ah, Death has the greatest
  purport.
WALT WHITMAN

In March, 1949, Antonis Kambanis turned fifty years old, and for the first time in years he decided to celebrate his birthday at home with friends, Basil tidied the house and cooked yiouvetsi, following the instructions of his paralyzed mother, then just before nine Arsen showed up with dessert, and a few minutes later the bell rang and Antonis's friends from the Niagara coffee house came in, the owner Mikis with his overweight wife Maro, Lakis from Volos and his best friend Makis from Kozani, both handsome and always dressed to the nines but for some inexplicable reason still unmarried, and around nine-thirty the Levantine seamstress Lenio arrived late, and knowing that there would be two single men at the party she brought along a lovely, lively firecracker from Smyrna named Tasoula who came with her young daughter in tow. Tasoula was also an old friend of Rallou's, she had left New Jersey for New York ten years earlier, but things there didn't work out quite as she had expected, her fiancé Vrasidas turned out to have been married all along and all his promises of a wedding, frills and frippery, a baptism for the baby and so on had gone to hell, so she'd packed up and slunk back to Camden with her tail between her legs. When all the guests were there Arsen raised his glass and made the first toast to their host's health and happiness, wishing Antonis Kambanis another half century of happy returns, a joyous hundredth birthday surrounded by grandkids, and since Rallou couldn't raise her glass, she avoided those first sips, which suited her just fine, she felt self-conscious around Tasoula and wanted tonight of all nights to keep her cool, and as everyone praised the food and the sweet, smooth wine, Rallou simply waited, lying there lame in her wheelchair in her best skirt and jacket, and everything was festive and bright and the guests full of compliments, but running her eyes around the room she saw things coolly and logically, saw the naked truth, the walls in need of painting, the cupboards dinged and flaking at the corners, Maro trying to hide her extra weight under a gigantic blouse, how Mikis avoided smiling and always covered his mouth when he spoke because of his rotten teeth, how Tasoula kept patting down her thinning hair, combing it with her fingers to keep it from flying all over the place, the way she made eyes at the two unmarried men as she ate, how Makis and Lakis snuck glances at one another when they thought no one was looking, they certainly didn't seem like great catches to Rallou, because she knew perfectly well what pretty boys like that could get up to, pretending to be Casanovas and ladies' men while they played footsie with one another under the table, she finally asked for a sip of wine, deciding that without the comfort of drink, without an impulse toward perversion or self-destruction the world was unbearable, and she instantly forgave everyone's pettiness and flaws and emptied the glass of wine they brought her in a single long sip, through a straw, and asked for a second and third, she wished everyone and everything would just go to hell, how much longer was she condemned to live, they were all sunk up to the waist in the same shit, and she was swimming in it too, frantically, aimlessly, even in her paralysis, and she called her son and Tasoula's daughter over, and while the others were busy praising the ravani Arsen had brought, Rallou pointed out the dust on the floor and the rusted hinges, Maro sneaking an extra piece of dessert, how Mikis chewed carefully because he was missing half his molars, the girl's flushed mother giggling and chirping like a goldfinch from her perch between Makis and Lakis, and that penny-pinching Arsen who, after he carefully cut and served the ravani, tucked the wrapper and bow from the box into his inside coat pocket, and she called out a toast, "Health and happiness to your future generations," because she believed with all the warmth of her heart in the continuation of this remarkable creature called man, and she started to laugh, almost choking with hilarity, "Here's to them," guffawing so uproariously that the blanket slipped off her wheelchair, leaving her ugly, gnarled, withered legs bare and exposed, and everyone's blood froze and an awkwardness and unease spread through the room like mist, and the evening ended there, with the guest's frozen smiles hanging in midair, and a few moments later they all headed toward the door in a disorderly exit, it was past three and Antonis Kambanis stood alone in the doorway for a long time, he had entered his fifty-first year on this planet and had no desire to go to sleep, he was waiting for something, something that would never arrive.

What did arrive two days later in an official brown envelope from the Immigration and Naturalization Service was his green card, the address smeared and smudged from the sudden morning rain, the paper had gotten wet and was slightly ripped, and his heart began to beat wildly with the agitation of his long anticipation, and for an instant he wished for the worst, but when he opened the envelope the laminated green card was sitting there untouched, staring him tauntingly in the face, the hair that had gone entirely gray, his sunken cheeks, little caves carved into his face where there had once been gentle hills and valleys, and on this official document under a different light in different conditions his own name seemed so strange to him, almost funny, the vowels leaping forward, pulling the consonants into a tangle, and he tossed the envelope in the trash and hid the green card in the drawer with a stack of unpaid bills and never mentioned it to anyone. At the shop that day he snapped at Arsen who was trying to save thread by counting Lenio's double stitching on the hems she was mending, and that evening he went to the Pole Vobrosky's restaurant with the strange name 44 and ordered a plate of golabki, but the food wouldn't go down, and that night at home, in front of their new television, bought on sale and on an installment plan for his fiftieth birthday, he turned it on, waited for the static to fade from the screen, and turned the knob to NBC so they could watch *You Bet Your Life!*—and as Groucho Marx teased the contestants and poked fun at his co-host George Fenneman's spotless, immaculate appearance, the clue came up in the geography category, "It was once known as Constantinople, but today it goes by a different name," and Antonis and Rallou silently shook their heads, the answer sitting unspoken in their mouths for the past twenty-six years, and after the final 10,000-dollar question, "Is it possible to be in two places at once?" Rallou thought it over glancingly and Basil barely at all, he wasn't interested in quiz shows, but Kambanis wracked his brain for the answer, and in the end they agreed that it wasn't possible, it was clearly humanly impossible, and Groucho shook his head and wagged a finger and told them they should have considered it more carefully, of course it's possible, "You can be in two places at once if you straddle the border of two states," or two countries, for that matter, if one foot is in Arkansas and the other in Oklahoma, one in America and the other in Canada, "and hence, my dears, the phrase one foot in the grave,"

Groucho joked, winking at them slyly, reminding everyone of their eventual final destination.

On September 6, 1949, Antonis Kambanis got up and made coffee, his back was bothering him and he hadn't slept well, he looked at his watch which showed eight-thirty and he let Rallou sleep a little longer, flipped through a pile of cancelled orders and made a note for himself about his afternoon appointment at the bank, he planned on closing the stores, he'd been trying to find a buyer for six months but his asking price was too high, no one wanted to invest in repairs and alterations, times had changed and he was being put out to pasture yet again, he was in danger of going belly-up, his bank account was on a steady decline and he was hounded by growing debts, his income barely covered operating expenses, taxes were crushing him, the decks were stacked against him, these days when things got old people just tossed them in the trash, and as he was walking to the shop, moving on autopilot, shortly after nine he heard something that sounded like gunfire but surely wasn't, he took it for the distant sound of a noisy motorcycle trying in vain to start, or an exhaust pipe backfiring, then he heard a second and third noise that seemed a bit closer but still couldn't be gunshots, and he paid no attention, passed by a parked truck whose wide-open door oozed a dozen bottles of spilled milk, then picked up his pace to the corner, and as he turned he suddenly saw the scene, two bodies lying awkwardly on the sidewalk in a pool of blood, and a man in a bow tie and white suit aiming at him from medium range in the middle of the street, and a fourth bullet whizzed right by him and as he ran for his life he began to faint, fell flat on his face on the ground, felt the ground melting away beneath his feet, and with all the life left in his body he opened his mouth to say something timely and relevant, but he couldn't remember how everything had begun, so as to pick up the story from the start.

XIX

spring wind frees
the full moon tangled
in leafless trees
NICK VIRGILIO

Antonis Kambanis tucks into a slice of cake covered
in icing and flecks of white chocolate, he's gotten it
all over his mouth and his striped pajamas, but
today the nurse doesn't scold him, it's his birthday,
and birthdays are the one occasion, aside from
Thanksgiving and Christmas, when the staff at the
Hope Nursing Home is willing to turn a blind eye
and overlook health department regulations, in fact
the plump nurse with the nametag reading *Gladys*
on her lapel brought a little transistor radio and
tuned it to a station playing salsa and merengue,
and though she doesn't speak a word of Spanish, she
keeps singing along softly to the love songs, "How
old are you today, honey?" she asks, but Antonis
doesn't look up, just uses his fork to spear a spongy
morsel of chocolate cake, feeding himself is quite a

feat with his trembling hands and lips, a constant struggle against his own body, his roommate Vince left them a week ago, took off for his final resting place where he's now pushing up daisies, his bed is empty, impeccably made up with crisp, clean sheets—for three days Antonis's eyes kept wandering to the bed next to him, something was missing but he didn't know what, until he got used to the absence and on the fourth day everything was just as before. Gladys takes the empty plate from his hands and replaces the cheap leather slipper that's dropped from his right foot, his crooked, yellowed toenails look like the claws of some creature that's walked days and nights over fallen leaves and fresh soil in search of food and shelter, and his puzzled gaze follows the plate that is no longer in his possession, his frozen hands now grasping empty air, and they'll stay like that until Gladys gives them something else to do or finds a way to calm them, and with nothing to offer in place of the plate, she puts her own hands in his for a bit, time is a hazy landscape that's pushed itself layer by layer into an always unfinished painting, and as Antonis struggles to remember why two hands would ever be holding one another, Gladys thinks back to the days when he first came to live there, he was younger, almost healthy, in his late 60s or early 70s, he'd lost his wife to a heart attack three years before and the first signs of Parkinson's had just begun to appear.

Antonis Kambanis had managed to sell the Parkside storefront to a down-at-the-heels Mexican, but lost the other location to taxes, interest, and debt, his friend Mikis had advised him to put the money from the sale to good use, to buy a house in the suburbs and get out while there was still time, in a few years the neighborhood would be filled with all kinds of riff-raff, blacks, yellows, browns who didn't speak the language but still demanded work and equal opportunities, the city of Camden was going from bad to worse, all the respectable white neighbors were leaving in droves, Mikis himself had gotten nervous about the rising number of blacks, had closed the taps of the Niagara and relocated to Cherry Hill, and Antonis Kambanis was thinking of doing the same with the money he'd set aside, buying his family a house with a yard outside of town, but when Basil told him he hoped to get married and move out pretty soon, Antonis Kambanis suddenly felt lost and confused about the future, what would two old people do in a big, hulking house out in the middle of nowhere, how would they pass the time, whatever days and years were left to them? His son had set his sights on marriage, and once he'd made up his mind he lost no time in making it happen, found a ready-made family, a woman with a little girl, married her and moved one neighborhood down, a half-hour by foot from his parents' house, and made a life with Susan and Leto—and with that, his mother Rallou was released from all earthly obligations, took her marching orders for the skies, and a few months later died quietly in her sleep, having nodded off in her wheelchair in front of the television one afternoon, and when Basil came by three hours later he found her unmoving, unspeaking, in the exact same position, a slight woman with white hair and a smattering of white whiskers on her upper lip and chin who exuded peace and kindness in death, a stranger to him, a stranger who resembled yet was not his mother.

After Rallou died, Antonis became convinced that his own time was near, and he asked Basil if he could move in with his family, he didn't want to die alone, and in return he'd hand over all his savings, a bank account with a few thousand dollars, plus his monthly retirement check. Basil and Susan talked it over and agreed, they moved Antonis in and started to look for a bigger house and a business to call their own, prices were good in Camden, and if for a moment they hesitated, it was because of the size of the house, three bedrooms and two baths with a yard and garage in Dudley, but in the end they bought it, set the grandfather up on the ground floor and Leto in the kids' room where Susan painted elephants and lions on the walls. They took out a commercial loan and set to work on their plan to open a diner, and under their care the old 44 became the Ariadne, where Susan, inspired by the faded portrait of the poet Mickiewicz on the wall, wanted to add a round 68 to the neon sign to honor that 44, but it didn't fit, and for days she kept trying to figure out some solution, she had her heart set on folding some meaningful number into their lives, and no matter how hard Basil tried to convince her that 1968 had been a mess of a year they'd just as soon forget, Susan remained adamant, she had a desperate need to hold on to something from her past and 1968 had nearly changed the world, for a moment in the arms of Scott and peyote she really believed the world was on the verge of becoming just a bit better, and while everything was chugging along according to plan, one day Antonis Kambanis lost his footing and fell down the stairs, breaking an arm and a hip, and as his health started to take a turn for the worse, they too began to lose their way—and no matter how many times he's climbed those stairs to the second floor of the Hope Nursing Home in the twelve years since, Basil always counts them, twenty-two steps, twenty-two, not one more or less, and he always has his hands in his pockets, feeling the same unease about the months that have passed since his last visit, about the house he bought with his father's money and the promises he failed to keep, the lies he told himself, about the nurse who asks Antonis Kambanis every time, as if she herself doesn't know, who's come to see him, who's that man standing in the door, does he remind Antonis of anyone, how are they related, and Antonis looks and sees nothing, his gaze has been vacant for years, his hands shake and his lips are just a thin line, drooping a bit on one side, weighed down by unfinished thoughts and unspoken words, and Basil Kambanis starts to open his mouth, to say "Dad," or maybe "Happy birthday," but there's no point anymore, and they all stand there silently, awkwardly arranged in space and time, and outside it is snowing, and soon the snow will cover everything, the guilt, passions, and suffering, the streets, the mistakes, and Gladys runs to close a window someone left open where cold air is rushing in, but the window is stubborn and won't go down, the hinges are old, the nuts and bolts have come loose, the wood has warped, and outside it is snowing, and now it is snowing inside, too, a heavy snow, and no matter how hard Gladys tries, soon enough that snow will cover them all.

XX

SNOWFLAKE BENTLEY MUSEUM, JERICHO, VERMONT

"… Under the microscope, I found that snowflakes were miracles of beauty; and it seemed a shame that this beauty should not be seen and appreciated by others. Every crystal was a masterpiece of design and no one design was ever repeated. When a snowflake melted, that design was forever lost. Just that much beauty was gone, without leaving any record behind. I became possessed with a great desire to show people something of this wonderful loveliness, an ambition to become, in some measure, its preserver …"

Author's Acknowledgements

I would like to personally thank Father Emmanuel Prat-sinakis and the St. Thomas Greek Orthodox Church in Cherry Hill, New Jersey, for sharing historical materials relating to the Greek community in Camden and for their prompt responses to my inquiries.

I would also particularly like to thank Katerina Schina for her advice.

Krystalli for her help.

Penny and my sister for their late-night conversations and support.

Translator's Acknowledgements

Many thanks are due to Kallia Papadaki for writing such a beautiful book, for her kind patience in answering my questions, and for the graciousness with which she endured my obsessive fact-checking of a fictional work. I am also grateful to Lydia Unsworth of World Editions for her impeccable and inspired editing.

The staff at the Snowflake Bentley Museum was kind enough to locate the source and share the precise word-ing in English of the final passage in the book; it is a quo-tation from William "Snowflake" Bentley contained in a 1925 article about him by Mary B. Mullet, which can be found on the *Resources* page of the museum's website. The epigraph to the book, from W.G. Sebald's *The Rings of Saturn*, is quoted here in Michael Hulse's translation. And the haiku by Danielle Murdoch that serves as the epigraph to Chapter IX, cited in the Greek text in a translation by Krystalli Glyniadaki, was originally published on the website of the Haiku Society of America, as part of its 2013 Student Haiku Awards in Memorial of Nicholas A. Virgilio.

   As always, thanks go to Panayiotis Pantzarelas and Andreas Galanos, my lifelong partners in reading. And to my parents, Helen and David Emmerich, for everything.

KAREN EMMERICH is a translator of modern Greek literature and an Associate Professor of Comparative Literature at Princeton University. Her translation awards include the National Translation Award for Ersi Sotiropoulos's *What's Left of the Night*, the Best Translated Book Award for Eleni Vakalo's *Beyond Lyricism*, and the PEN Poetry in Translation Award for Yannis Ritsos's *Diaries of Exile* (co-translated with Edmund Keeley). She lives in Brooklyn.

Book Club Discussion Guides on our website.

World Editions promotes voices from around the globe by publishing books from many different countries and languages in English translation. Through our work, we aim to enhance dialogue between cultures, foster new connections, and open doors which may otherwise have remained closed.

Also available from World Editions:

Emily Forever
Maria Navarro Skaranger
Translated by Martin Aitken
A novel about poverty, social inequality, and class contempt in Norway.

Afterlight
Jaap Robben
Translated by David Doherty
This moving novel gives voice to the silent grief of the mothers of stillborn children.

Selamlik
Khaled Alesmael
Translated by Leri Price
An unflinching story about Arab masculinity and homoeroticism.

Where the Wind Calls Home
Samar Yazbek
Translated by Leri Price
"The potent latest from Yazbek weighs the consequences of the Syrian civil war. This slim novel packs a punch." —*Publishers Weekly*

On the Isle of Antioch
Amin Maalouf
Translated by Natasha Lehrer
"A beguiling, lyrical work of speculative fiction by a writer of international importance."
—*Kirkus Reviews*, *Starred Review*

On the Design

As book design is an integral part of the reading experience, we would like to acknowledge the work of those who shaped the form in which the story is housed.

Tessa van der Waals (Netherlands) is responsible for the cover design, cover typography, and art direction of all World Editions books. She works in the internationally renowned tradition of Dutch Design. Her bright and powerful visual aesthetic maintains a harmony between image and typography, and captures the unique atmosphere of each book. She works closely with internationally celebrated photographers, artists, and letter designers. Her work has frequently been awarded prizes for Best Dutch Book Design.

The background image resembling a body of water was shot by Paweł Czerwiński, a photographer based in Poland who specializes in experimental photography.

The typeface used for the title on the cover is FF Supergrotesk, created by German type designer Svend Smital in 1999. It was chosen for its boldness and its striking capital E. The Neutraface font used for the author name was designed and published by House Industries, and named after the architect Richard Neutra.

The cover has been edited by lithographer Bert van der Horst of BFC Graphics (Netherlands).

Euan Monaghan (United Kingdom) is responsible for the typography and careful interior book design.

The text on the inside covers and the press quotes are set in Circular, designed by Laurenz Brunner (Switzerland) and published by Swiss type foundry Lineto.

All World Editions books are set in the typeface Dolly, specifically designed for book typography. Dolly creates a warm page image perfect for an enjoyable reading experience. This typeface is designed by Underware, a European collective formed by Bas Jacobs (Netherlands), Akiem Helmling (Germany), and Sami Kortemäki (Finland). Underware are also the creators of the World Editions logo, which meets the design requirement that "a strong shape can always be drawn with a toe in the sand."

Printed in the USA
CPSIA information can be obtained
at www.ICGtesting.com
JSHW022340140724
66374JS00008B/3